The Dance

KAYE SPENCER

LASTERDAY STORIES, LLC

The Dance
1st Ed. novelette Copyright© 2010 Kaye Spencer
2nd Ed. novella Copyright© 2025 Kaye Spencer
Cover design – Kaye Spencer

Published by LasterdayStories, LLC
www.lasterdaystories.com
All rights reserved.

ISBN: 979-8-9997445-1-7
Library of Congress Control Number: 2025916943

To everyone who has ever
been afraid to risk their heart for love.

Chapter One

Denver, Colorado – October 12, 1999

Out of patience and working against a deadline, Janae Palmer hit the delete key on her keyboard too hard, which sent it skittering across the floor. She seldom lost her temper, and even more rarely did she hear her upstairs neighbor, but ten minutes ago he'd cranked up his music past noise ordinance regulations, and it wasn't letting up. With Mr. Cowboy Way literally dancing on her ceiling, it was impossible to concentrate on her book review.

Searching on hands and knees, she found the flyaway key under the bookshelf too far back to reach. Flicking and swiping with a ruler, she worked the key toward her.

Perturbed as she was at the racket overhead, it did nothing to dampen the fact that Owen Quinlan was a good-looking guy in an earthy, tight-fitting jeans, redneck sort of way—six-foot something with jet-black, wavy hair and sky blue, let's get naked eyes. The first time she'd seen him was etched in her memory—August 31st. It was the day she'd moved into her apartment. Every day since, fantasizing about him had occupied much of her nights and a fair share of her waking hours. As such, each time they met, she hurried on with only a mumbled hello for fear he'd read the interest in her eyes.

Their only conversation had occurred last week when they'd picked up their mail at the same time. She'd not meant to stare, but he was raw, male sex personified clad in form-fitting, wet swim trunks with a towel draped around his shoulders. He'd dropped an envelope, and she'd stooped to retrieve it only to gape wide-eyed at his crotch, unable to draw her gaze away for several long seconds.

Embarrassed at her shameless gawking and doubly horrified that it amused him, she'd flushed head to toe, stammering inanely that the envelope appeared to be a medical bill. His cryptic explanation of an injury at an Oklahoma rodeo last spring had sent her on a newspaper article search. She discovered he was a rodeo clown, but not just any rodeo clown. He was, or had been, a professional rodeo bullfighter ranked in the all-time top ten of rodeo protection athletes until a broken back had sidelined him.

Since that mortifying mailbox encounter, she'd read his blog, *Rodeo Reflections from a Bull's Eye View*, so often she practically knew every word by heart. The article about his injuries fascinated her. His back was broken in three places. Although his spinal cord wasn't damaged, nerve trauma was the healing challenge.

He'd explained he had a high pain threshold, which helped him not become dependent on pain medication once he'd left the hospital and gone into a rehab facility. He'd written that he hadn't come out of the rehab facility pain-free, but he was usually able to manage his pain with over-the-counter meds and an occasional shot of whiskey, although not at the same time. He only took prescription pain killers and muscle relaxants as a last resort. Janae marveled at his self-determination to overcome his initial lower body paralysis.

In her infatuation, she'd scoured library archives for old newspapers and magazines and had spent hours at the microfiche machine to find everything and anything she could about him. She'd hit the jackpot with a Denver Sunday newspaper feature celebrating the 100th anniversary of the Quinlan ranch and their contribution to rodeo over the years. She immediately made an Internet map search to locate his hometown of Overland Crossing, which she discovered was an hour and a half drive east of Denver on Interstate 76. The ranch headquarters were another twenty minutes north of town.

To say she had a colossal crush on Owen Quinlan was an understatement. As long as he didn't know it, though, her fantasies couldn't be ruined by two realities: First, guys like Owen never looked twice at ordinary women like her, and second, that she harbored a distaste for rodeo in general.

She snagged the delete key just as the music stopped, snapped the key back into place, and settled at her desk. Her short-lived respite vanished with renewed foot-stomping and a pounding bass beat coming through her ceiling.

Exasperated, she pushed back, stubbed her toe on the desk leg, and spilled her uncapped bottle of seltzer water over the desktop. Hastily sopping up the mess, she grabbed her key lanyard, slipped it around her neck, and hop-walked to the door, slamming it behind her. She hobbled along the hallway to the central stairway, all the while grumbling disparagingly about the legitimacy of his birth.

With her flip-flop sandals slapping smartly against her heels and her hair bouncing at her shoulders with every irate step, she stormed up the flight of stairs, hurried along the hallway, and knocked on his door. No response. She paced, wondering why she was the only one here to complain. It was impossible to ignore the obscene lyrics about a guy driving a truck to a rodeo in subzero weather. She was convinced the song was stuck on repeat, which made it all the more dreadful to endure.

She had no personal experience with cowboys, but if Owen Quinlan was representative of the species, the lot of them were as uncouth as they were uncivilized—the drop-dead gorgeous ones not excepted.

She knocked again. What was he doing in there? Kicking cow shit? Beyond frustrated, she twisted the doorknob and shoved. The door swung wide, propelling her across the threshold amidst a jumble of flying foam flip-flops. In her fumbling, she stepped on the hem of her ankle-length gauze skirt, managed to stumble into her sandals, and then forged onward like a rider in Tennyson's light brigade.

And abruptly stopped.

Owen Quinlan stood with his back to her. Shirtless. The scar running the length of his spine captivated her with macabre fascination. Slowly lowering her gaze, she lingered on the way he fit into his jeans before lifting her gaze to appreciate the bronzed, defined muscles of his broad shoulders that simply begged caressing...

Reaching out, she smoothed her hands along his biceps and over his shoulders then tickled her fingers up his neck and buried her fingers in his hair. Pressing her body to his back, she encircled his waist with her arms and skimmed her palms across his belly on the way to undo the button on his jeans. She dragged the zipper pull down, teasing her fingers—

Owen joining in with the song's raucous chorus jolted her from her daydream. With a sweeping glance, she took stock of the room. A corner console had a television set with VHS tapes stacked five high beside it on the top shelf. A boom box with CDs were wedged in the middle shelf. *Scrabble, Yahtzee,* and *Battleship* games filled the bottom shelf with *UNO* and a deck of cards wedged along one side. The desktop was just barely large enough for a computer, printer, and cordless phone. Rodeo photographs were tacked to walls with paintings arranged neatly along the baseboards. A folding card table held a partially completed puzzle.

Bringing her perusal back to Owen, her notion of a cowboy abruptly clashed with the canvas and easel on the drop cloth in front of him, the long-handled, slender brush in his left hand, and the painter's palette balanced in his right. Shaking off this visual contradiction, she barged across the room and tapped Owen on the shoulder just as the words to the hideously awful song faded.

"Excuse me."

"*Shit!*" Owen whipped around. "What the—?"

She saw the palette swinging too late.

A phantom-like voice wavered at the fringes of her twilight awareness, talking to her, calling her name, urging her to wake up. Wake up? No. She was happy where she was...

Owen untied the last ribbon of her black negligee and watched it slide off her shoulders to heap at her feet. He took her hands and pulled her down to straddle his body as he lay back on the red satin sheets. She crooned his name between the kisses she placed across his chest as she moved lower—

"Janae. Wake up."

The tap on her cheek was as harsh as his voice, and both wrenched her from her private reverie. She came to a slow awareness of lying on the carpet with a cloth over her face and nose. She lifted her hands to touch it.

"Hold still. Your nose is bleeding. The pressure you feel is an ice bag wrapped in a towel. Your glasses have seen better days, but it doesn't look like your nose is broken. I don't think I hit you hard enough to give you a concussion. No. Leave the ice bag where it is."

Bleeding? Swelling? Concussion?

Janae jerked into coherency. The sharp pain between her eyes brought the recollection of the palette-to-glasses blow. Owen folded the edge of the towel from her eyes.

"How're you doing?"

Janae closed one eye to bring his face into focus so only one mustache framed one set of lips. "I don't know. My face hurts. How long was I unconscious?"

"You were never clear out, just dazed for the last..." He checked his watch. "Couple of minutes, give or take."

"That's vague— Are you checking my pulse?" The towel and ice bag plopped on the carpet when she looked.

"Yep." He released her wrist and flashed a pen light into her eyes. "Pupils are good. Pulse is strong, but a little fast, as expected under the circumstances." He stuffed the pen light into his back pocket. "What day is it?"

"Wednesday, why?"

He nodded. "What's your apartment number?"

"2G."

"Phone number?"

"Three—" She caught herself. "This is not the most propitious moment to ask for my phone number. In fact, it's a rather boorish and formulaic pick-up line which I don't appreciate."

"Nothing wrong with your orientation." He chuckled. "I'm an emergency medical technician. EMT."

"I know. You're also a rodeo clown." How stupid that sounded. It seemed she had no control over the communication between her brain and mouth, and she wondered what other nonsense she'd babbled.

He cocked an eyebrow. "I don't recall us talking about this."

"That time in the mail room when you dropped the envelope, you said you were injured in a rodeo accident. I found your website."

"Good to know someone reads it." He grinned. "How'd you get in here?"

"Your door was unlocked."

"Oh, yeah." He glanced absently at the door. "I only lock it when I'm gone and then not every time. Habit from growing up in the country." Eyeing her curiously, he said, "You could've at least brought a bottle of wine. Here. Take a drink of water."

He helped her sit up and gave her a glass of water that she gratefully accepted. She handed the glass to him, and he put it on the coffee table.

"Better?"

She nodded. "Yes."

"Why did you sneak up on me, and what do you want?"

"My boss is a stickler about deadlines, and it was impossible to work with the commotion you were making."

She pressed her fingers around her eyes and over her nose in a gentle typing motion to test for tender places. "You really don't think my nose is broken?"

"I don't, but if you're worried, I'll call Roger. He'll drive you to the ER."

"Maybe I should—"

What was she thinking? This might be the only opportunity she'd ever have to be alone with Owen. Silencing the screaming hypochondriac in her head, she said, "Maybe I'll just rest here a bit, if you don't mind."

"I don't mind at all. I'll get you a couple of ibuprofens. It's all I've got."

"Oh, thank you, but no. I'm allergic to it. I'll take acetaminophen when I go back to my apartment."

"Are you allergic to whiskey?"

"Excuse me?"

"Are you allergic to whiskey?"

She gaped at him. "You're offering me alcohol after I've taken a blow to the face? Isn't that contradictory to some critical EMT guideline?"

His eyes shined with mischief. "It would be if it wasn't the famous Owen Quinlan remedy for punching a woman in the nose and having her collapse on the living room floor then finding out she has an allergy to the only non-prescription pain meds he has on hand."

"Occurs frequently, does it?" Smiling hurt.

With pseudo-seriousness, he said, "I'm beginning to suspect that's the reason I don't get repeat dates." He stood and extended his arms. "I'd have carried you to my bed—couch—" He squinted on a grimace.

Bed? Janae perked up.

"But I'm supposed to baby my back a couple more months. It's literally held together with screws, wire mesh, and a steel rod. Here. Take my hands. Let's get you off the floor." He wiggled his fingers for her to grab hold.

Chapter Two

J anae's knees buckled under the instant head rush. Owen caught her in his arms, which sent a warm flush coursing through her body.

"Hey, don't pass out on me again." He guided her to the couch. "You'll have a couple of shiners by morning. I'm sorry about your glasses." He gave her the broken frames with one popped-out lens. "Hope you aren't too blind without them."

"I'll get by. I have another pair of glasses. I have anisometropia. I usually wear contact lenses. I'm as significantly nearsighted in one eye as I am farsighted in the other." *Why am I babbling? He doesn't care about my vision diagnosis.*

"You have what?"

"Anisometropia." She wished her brain and mouth would get back in sync so her inane chatter would stop.

His mustache twitched with a suppressed grin. "Does that go along with having a glass jaw? You dropped like a rock."

Irked at his teasing, but not irked enough to leave, Janae made a face, then awkwardly balanced the towel and ice bag over her face. Owen chuckled as he walked away. A few seconds later, she heard cabinet doors open and close then the chink of glass on glass.

Lifting the towel, she peered at the blood on it then gingerly touched her nose with the tips of her fingers, wincing at the soreness. Sitting up, she tilted her head back and held the towel to her nostrils. From the corner of her eye, she watched Owen coming toward her, his sleeves rolled halfway to his elbows and his shirt hanging open, which framed a tantalizing view of the black, curly hair on his broad chest. So help her, she tingled all over at the sight.

He held out a glass with an inch of whiskey and two ice cubes in it.

"It's a smooth bourbon. It'll go down like warm honey."

"No, thank you."

"Is your nose throbbing?"

"Of course."

"Then drink this. It'll take the edge off."

Holding the glass like it was something filthy, she sniffed, made a face, then took a petite sip, grimacing at the flavor.

Owen sat in the upholstered chair opposite the coffee table between them and set the whiskey bottle on the table. Looking her over, he said. "So, you've got a glass jaw and you drink like a girl. Take it like this." He tossed his off in a gulp followed by a satisfied *mmm*.

A glistening drop of whiskey lingered on his bottom lip. She scooted across the coffee table to touch it. Playing his tongue around her finger, he sucked it into his mouth. She moaned on a breathless sigh. He laid her down to the coffee table, bunched her skirt around her waist, and kissed the inside of her knee, slowly working his way along her inner thigh—

Owen snapped his fingers. "Hey, Janae."

She jumped and fumbled the glass, barely righting it before it sloshed.

"You spaced out for a second. Maybe you do have a concussion. I'll call an ambulance. Mountain View Hospital's not far."

"N-n-no. I'm fine. I was just preoccupied for...for a moment." She gulped the whiskey. Gasping, eyes watering, she croaked, "You're normally quiet. Why was your music so loud?" She took a swallow of water to wash away the whiskey taste. It didn't work.

"My headphones gave up the ghost, and I haven't been anywhere to buy new ones. I must have been absorbed in what I was painting. The spirit moved me." He laughed.

"You are delusional and tone-deaf if you believe that cacophonous clamor was music."

"You know, you throw vocabulary around like a weapon, which reminds me of several things I've noticed about you since you moved in."

Wary of where this was going, she asked, "Oh? Do tell."

"I'll bet you're a meditating, vitamin-chugging, incense-burning sort. Roger told me you recycle."

"Roger is a busybody."

"He sure is, and that makes him a damn good apartment manager. He's friendly, observant, and helpful, but back to my point. You drive one of the most environmentally efficient compact cars on the market, which coincidentally also has a high road safety rating, and you carry your groceries in Earth-friendly, reusable bags."

She countered, "There's nothing wrong with being environmentally conscientious."

He waved her off. "Mother Earth will get rid of humans before she lets us do serious damage to her. I've also seen you at the pool. Your skin is creamy white, which means you don't sunbathe or go to a tanning bed, because you're mindful of skin cancer. It wouldn't hurt you to get some good old-fashioned fresh air and sunshine on your...cheeks."

He half-pointed at her as if undecided which cheeks he meant. His grin at his double entendre wasn't lost on her, but she didn't show it.

"I take care of myself. It's important to live a healthy lifestyle."

"I don't disagree, but preserving yourself until you end up in a nursing home regretting what you missed out on isn't living. Hunter S. Thompson said something to the effect that if you arrive at the end of your life in good shape instead of worn out and used up, then your ride through life was a wasted journey."

"Hunter S. Thompson lives in an alternate reality. If you're insinuating that I hide from life, you're mistaken. I do...things."

"Predictable things. You get in your car at seven-thirty on Monday, Wednesday, and Thursday. You're back in time to attend the five-thirty yoga session in the fitness room on Monday. You're home around twelve-thirty on Wednesday.

"You don't leave your apartment on Tuesday or Friday or Wednesday afternoon. It's not rocket science to figure out you go to a day job two-and-a-half days and work from home the other days. You shop once a week after work on Thursday, and you're typically home by six- thirty—and you bring take-out.

"You swim Saturday and Sunday mornings. You don't leave in your car on weekends, but you usually go out walking. Maybe to the zoo or Museum of Natural History. They're both close."

Janae smiled and nodded that he was correct.

"You moved in at the end of August. You haven't had a single visitor. You don't order food for delivery. You don't go out in the evenings. That seems like a lukewarm existence and lonely and boring as hell."

"Did Roger tell you all this about me?"

He grinned. "With an occasional six-pack and pizza, Roger keeps me informed on what I miss. Plus, our apartments are at the end of our floors. We have corner windows overlooking the courtyard and parking lot. When you're looking for anything to help pass the time while you're stuck in the city like I've been for half a year, those two windows are sanity-savers."

Janae pursed her lips, trying not to smile. "Our corner windows do offer voyeuristic opportunities, which means two can play this game. From what you've put on your blog, and what I've deduced and witnessed, every Thursday morning, you walk to and from your therapy at a rehab facility, which is affiliated with the hospital where you had surgery. You swim Monday, Wednesday, Friday, and Saturday mornings. You work out in the gym on Tuesday morning, and you often go for short walks in the park, or you sit in the courtyard for the sunshine. I think you rest on Sunday. You purposely live on the third floor for the added exercise of the stairs."

Owen inclined his head in agreement. "Don't stop now. What else?"

"I've never seen you carrying groceries, but I have seen grocery deliveries taken to the third floor. It's not unreasonable to presume they are for you. You don't go out at night, either, and you don't have a vehicle. As for visitors, your family drives vehicles with *Quinlan Rodeo Stock Contractor, Inc.* painted on the doors. It's impossible not to notice when they come to see you, which is most often on weekends."

Owen stretched out his legs. "It seems we share mutual curiosity about each other."

"Yes, it does."

Owen's attention seemed to turn inward. He stared toward the easel, but she didn't think he was necessarily looking at it. The silence that followed made Janae uncomfortable. Was he bored? Should she go? She'd never been any good at table-talk, as her mother called it.

Still off somewhere in his thoughts, Owen asked, "Are you satisfied with your life?"

"Um... I suppose so. That came out of the blue. What prompted you to ask?"

"I was thinking about my family coming to see me just about every week, and I haven't been home in months. The waiting gets me down sometimes, and I get to feeling sorry for myself for no good reason. This is only temporary.

"Even if I could physically tolerate riding in a vehicle for any length of time, it's too far to drive into Denver from the ranch to get the daily therapy I need. Plus, my doctor and therapists are wise not to trust me to stay off horses and away from bulls. They know me too well." He shrugged off whatever memories were behind those words.

"You've also written on your blog that you're making better and quicker progress than expected. So that's another positive."

"It is. You're right. I'll be out of here soon enough and back to my normal life, or as close to normal as a healed broken back allows."

"Normal life means rodeo?"

"Yeah."

"Isn't that risky enough when you don't have a broken back?"

"I like risky."

"Obviously."

"What was the last risky thing you did?"

She thought for a minute. "I wouldn't call it risky, but moving here from my hometown of Kent, Ohio was exciting."

"First time away from home?"

"That depends on how you define 'away from home'."

"Not living with your parents. Having your own place."

"Then, no. I've lived by myself."

"I'll bet it was in the dorm or an apartment down the street from Mom and Dad."

His smug teasing irritated her.

"It's perfectly natural to be close to your parents when you're an only child."

"Evidently so. Roger mentioned your parents—Vic and Ramona—and usually Ramona, call him if you don't answer your apartment phone or your cell phone when they think you should. That's either massive control on their part or extreme insecurity on yours."

Indignant and defensive, she shot back, "Roger needs to mind his own business. Aren't you close to your parents?"

"And my sisters, grandparents, cousins, aunts, and uncles, but I don't talk to them every day."

"Then I'm sorry for you. Maybe you should talk to your family more often. You shouldn't take your family for granted. You never know when it will be too late."

Her words stopped whatever he was going to say. He sat back, muttering, "You're not the first to tell me that." He went quiet for a few seconds as he stared into his empty glass, then he shook off whatever was on his mind.

"Putting that aside, another thing I know about you is we have different tastes in music. I'll bet your musical taste leans toward New Age and easy-listening.

"Just because my vocabulary consists of larger-than-four-letter words, and I happen to appreciate emotionally nurturing music, doesn't grant you the liberty to make judgments about my life or my lifestyle."

"What about Marty or Willie?"

Janae shook her head. "I don't know who they are."

His eyebrows shot up. "Don't tell me you don't like Johnny Cash. Everyone likes Johnny Cash."

She wrinkled her nose.

"Who do you like?"

"Beethoven and Mozart. Tchaikovsky. Brahms. Some operas."

"I don't know anything about opera, but I agree with you on Beethoven, Mozart, Tchaikovsky, and Brahms. I'm partial to Liszt. Those were composers with big brass *cojones*."

In spite of herself, she giggled. "You are a crude man at times, Owen Quinlan."

A broad smile spread across his face. "I've mellowed. You should have known me before I broke my back."

She dabbed the towel to her nose and was pleased at the absence of fresh blood. "Speaking of your broken back, what you do—or did—as a rodeo clown is terrifying. I don't understand how anyone can do that."

Owen poured another inch of whiskey into his glass, gulped it, then set the glass and bottle aside. Shrugging, he said, "It's part of the job. This isn't the first time I've been banged-up by a bull. And it won't be the last."

The cordless phone on his desk rang. He walked to it, checked the number, then spoke over his shoulder to Janae. "Make yourself at home. This may take a while."

Phone to his ear, he said, "Hello, Laurel. I'm doing good. How are you?" Seconds passed as he listened, his smile widening. "And how're my boys? I haven't seen them since school started. Are you purposely keeping them from me? Do we have to go to court so I get regular visitation?"

Janae choked on a swallow of water. *He has children?*

Chapter Three

Owen howled at Laurel's response. "Don't get your panties in a wad. I was joking. Living in Denver is the shits. I'm itching to be home."

Thunderstruck, Janae stared at him. It hadn't crossed her mind that he might have a family...and a wife...or an ex-wife...or an estranged wife. In her fantasies, he was single and available, even though she'd never allowed herself to seriously entertain the possibility that available meant available to her.

Waving to get his attention, she whispered, "I'm leaving."

Shaking his head, he put his hand over the phone and said, "Stick around."

Up to now, fantasizing had been harmless. Pursuing a man with a family was not. This development made it all the more imperative to go. She placed the towel and ice bag on the coffee table.

Owen shook his head, mouthing *please don't leave*. Her conscience balked, but her suppressed adventurous side nudged her to stay. Surely, there was no harm in waiting until he got off the phone. It wasn't as if anything would happen between them, and it was awfully comfortable right there on his couch.

Closing her eyes against the dull headache, Janae still considered returning to her apartment for acetaminophen and to finish the book review since it was due before end of day tomorrow, but the headache wasn't conducive to writing a review about a scholarly book that had fallen wildly short of scholarly by any stretch of the imagination.

Her thoughts returned to contemplating Owen's marital status. Divorced or separated could account for why he hadn't seen his boys. She kicked herself for not noticing if he wore a wedding ring. Any self-respecting fantasizer would have looked for a ring right off. Trying not to be conspicuous, she cut a glance at his left hand. Darn it. Shoved in his pocket.

She made a cursory appraisal of the living room and of what she could see of the kitchen from her angle. The coat rack by the door held a wooden walking cane, denim jacket, blue baseball cap with *Quinlan Rodeo Stock Contractors, Inc.* embroidered in gold thread and arched over a likewise embroidered bucking bull. No family pictures, which struck her as odd, since he had sons. She could understand not displaying the mother's picture. A peek into his bedroom might reveal something more personal in that regard. She reasoned it wouldn't technically be snooping if she went to the bathroom to see what her face looked like and just happened to glance in his bedroom along the way.

While she ran a washcloth under warm water, she inspected her face in the mirror. The darkest bruising was right across the bridge of her nose. It took several re-wettings to remove the dried blood on her face and neck, but her blouse was hopelessly stained.

Satisfied she'd cleaned herself as best she could, she made a quick search of the bathroom drawers and medicine cabinet, but found only male toiletries, hot water bottle, electric heating pad, and bottles of prescription medications. She unscrewed the cap on the long neck of a bottle of aftershave and breathed in the heady aroma.

My God, this is a mating call in a bottle. The scent should be illegal.

She listened at the doorway, heard Owen talking, silenced her conscience, and stepped across the hallway into his bedroom. The room was neat and tidy. The accordion closet doors were open. Button-up shirts on hangers, a winter coat, and two pairs of dress pants took up a small bit of space. The pair of crutches beside the multi-colored crocheted afghan on the top shelf suggested he'd traded crutches for walking cane. Cowboy boots and athletic shoes were paired and lined up on the closet floor.

A light gray felt cowboy hat was perched on its crown on the dresser beside a small television set with built-in VHS player. She peeked in the drawers and found the clothing in them to be carefully folded and organized. Neat stacks of books and magazines graced the nightstand along with a cordless phone that matched the one he was talking on. Lifting the lid on the hamper, she saw his dirty clothes placed in layers rather than wadded and shoved inside.

A handmade quilt lay without a wrinkle over the mattress. She picked up one of the many pillows stacked at the headboard and breathed in his lingering scent. Holding the pillow to her body, she admired his tidiness, which was a contradiction to her presumption that men who lived alone were careless about housekeeping. At least there were no signs of a woman or children in his bedroom. Much as that pleased her, that he didn't have pictures of his kids was strange.

She replaced the pillow and returned to the living room. Having nothing to occupy herself while waiting, she looked at his paintings and photographs. Her perusal ended at the easel and canvas. For many moments, she studied the incomplete painting before she realized he was creating a color rendition from an eight-by-ten black and white photograph tacked to the wall beside the easel. The photograph captured the moment in time when a bucking bull charged a rodeo clown leaping to the aid of a cowboy tangled in the rope around the bull's girth. She recognized Owen under the grease paint, spandex, and baggy cut-off overalls that were held up by suspenders.

Owen strode into the room, alternately talking and listening as he paced. Janae's gaze went instantly to his left hand holding the phone.

No ring. She turned her face to conceal her smile.

"I saw on the news there'd been a microburst in town. Tore off part of the school's roof? Why didn't I know that? No school next week, either? Bring me a school calendar, will you? Laurel, it's the middle of October. Why are you talking about Thanksgiving? Oh, yeah. That makes sense. I forgot it'll be the day before Thanksgiving when they get back. All right. I promise I'll talk to Doc Harris about traveling home. You'll pick me up in the morning? Good. Bringing the boys? Great. Yeah. Appointment's at nine. Need to leave by eight-thirty. Doc's putting me through the works. Let's have lunch before you go back. Love you, too. Bye."

Of course he loves her. It's clear from his smile and voice. Whether separated or divorced, they appeared to have an amicable relationship, which meant the door was open for reconciliation. And why not? She's the mother of his children.

Janae's stomach knotted. Her throat closed against irrational disappointment. She desperately wished she'd gone to her apartment before hearing him say words of love to another woman. Feigning intense interest in his gallery, Janae went from one painting and photograph to the next, inching her way toward the door.

"Thanks for waiting. Oh, hey. Your face cleaned up pretty good. Sorry about your blouse." Owen entered a number on the phone. "I'm ordering supper. It's the least I can do for breaking your glasses, which I'll pay for, by the way."

"Oh, no. I couldn't accept payment, but thank you for offering."

She didn't trust herself to look directly at him for fear he'd see she was upset and ask why, when his personal life was none of her business.

"You like oriental?"

"No. It's full of artificial preservatives, and I'm allergic to M-S-G."

Eyeing her, he whistled softly, and muttered, "*Okaaay.*" He made another call.

"Owen. Really. I need to go."

"Why? Hot date tonight?"

She blushed. "No."

"Then you don't have an excuse to leave." He spoke into the phone. "Yeah— I need a number three, large and loaded. Mountain View Apartments on Colorado. Owen Quinlan in 3G. Yeah. Up the center stairs to the third floor. Hang a right. Go all the way to the end. Cash. Thanks." He looked at Janae as put the phone back on the charger. "Pizza'll be here in thirty minutes. I hope you're not a vegetarian...or vegan—whatever it's called. I ordered a thick crust meat supreme with extra cheese."

"I'm not vegan or vegetarian, and there is a difference, by the way. However, low-fat cheese on a thin wheat crust is a considerably healthier pizza, and I limit red meat."

He arched an eyebrow. "Yeah, that sounds appetizing as hell," he said drily. "Probably rivals the taste of cardboard. I'll stick with my unhealthy extra meaty-cheesy pizza."

She giggled at the awful face he made.

"I've been admiring your paintings." She indicated the partially completed one on the easel. "That's you, isn't it?"

He nodded. "When I broke my back. It was a wreck and a half. Jeff was hung up, but I got him loose. That bull and I danced before he hooked me. Jeff named his son after me—well sort of."

"What a charming tribute." Janae meant to be flippant. Owen didn't take it that way.

"Yeah, I thought so, too."

Janae was equal parts appalled and bewildered at the pride in his voice.

"This—" She waved at the painting. "It's terrifying. It's unmistakably the same scene as the photograph, but you've added something the photograph lacks." She shook her head, trying to voice her thoughts. "Something raw and elemental. Primeval. Man against nature. No. That's not it. Man against himself."

Owen nodded thoughtfully. "It's always man against beast in the arena, that's for sure."

"Well, I am impressed at your artistic talent. I can't draw recognizable stick figures. You should sell these."

Owen shrugged noncommittally. "My family says the same thing. I paint because it's therapeutic, not from a purely artistic need. Recovery is one-tenth physical and nine-tenths mental. When my head and hands aren't busy, I drive myself nuts wanting to get back to bullfighting."

"How can you even think about doing that? What if you're injured again?"

"In this profession, it's not a matter of if, but when and how bad."

"And you don't worry about that?"

"No. Never have. Never will."

"Not even with steel rods and screws and whatever else is in your back?"

"Steel mesh, and nope." He patted his right leg. "I don't have all the feeling back yet, but I will. Sometimes, I get a phantom pain off the end of my toes."

"I've read about that. It's typical of traumatic nerve damage."

"That's what my therapists tell me, and why I'm taking medication for nerve healing. When I'm overtired, I get a Walter Brennan limp, but I'm not crippled. Sitting too long with my knees bent, like riding in a car, is a killer. Things go numb. Well, more numb than usual. When the feeling comes back, it's like millions of hot needles jabbing me.

"Traveling's a problem. Can't go more than ten or fifteen minutes before I have to get out and walk around, but it's better than it was even a month ago. So, you see, I got off easy. The bull didn't kill me. I'm not paralyzed." He shrugged. "I know guys who weren't so lucky."

"I simply can't fathom how you face this." Janae indicated the photo.

He looked at her as if she'd grown another head. "What do you mean?"

"Why aren't you scared of worse injuries or even death if you return to being a rodeo clown?"

"The only thing that scares me is not being able to go back into the arena." He pondered the photo for several long seconds. "There are lots of reasons why I do what I do. There's nothing like the adrenaline rush when the bucking chute opens and a bull charges out, whether you're on its back or on the ground looking at it eye-to-eye. Getting between a bull and a cowboy, and helping that cowboy make it safely to the fence or to a pickup rider... It's... Well, there's not another feeling like it."

"That smacks of a thrill-seeking game of bull-tag at an unhealthy and, might I say, obsessive, level."

Chapter Four

"Bull-tag. I like it." He chuckled. "Never thought of it that way. I will admit to liking the thrill, but I'm not obsessed."

Janae frowned her skepticism.

"The real reason I keep doing what I do is because the cowboys tell me how much they appreciate me being there for them every time they sit down on a bull's back. I had a little girl call me her daddy's bodyguard one time." He chuckled. "There's an inside joke that we've saved more lives than the Secret Service."

"In essence, you're a human shield." She touched the bull in the photograph. "Against a thousand pounds of—"

"Two thousand, sometimes more."

"Against two thousand pounds of bucking bovine intent on crushing, killing, or maiming anyone and anything that gets in its way."

He nodded. "Yeah, that's about it."

"I think bull riders have a death wish, and this picture shows rodeo clowns share the same affliction."

He didn't quite grin. "That's a common misconception among non-rodeo people."

"If not a death wish, then what?"

"It's cheating Death to make it wait just a little longer. It's in my blood."

"Like an addiction?"

This time, he did grin. "Maybe not that extreme, but it's a passion, for sure. Talk to anyone serious in the profession, and they'll tell you the same thing. Once you get a taste, you want more. You crave it. It's you against your destiny every time that chute gate opens. I've been out of the arena for close to five months and there have been times I thought I'd lose my mind waiting to get back on the circuit."

"That's crazy. You're crazy. You should see a psychologist for counseling."

He laughed. "I am a psychologist."

She slapped her hands on her hips. "That seems farfetched."

"I went to college in Oklahoma on a rodeo scholarship and eventually had to choose a major. Psychology was interesting and didn't seem too difficult."

His grin and shrug were self-deprecating.

"Academics were secondary to rodeo until I graduated with an actual degree. I was proud of that accomplishment, despite the fact that an undergrad degree in psychology is worthless for getting a job." He chuckled. "I took that useless degree to a Colorado university and specialized in school psychology. My first, and only, job as a school psych was at a Denver County youth facility."

"Which is...?"

"Basically, jail for teens. I didn't like it. Incarceration isn't the way to help kids. It merely hones their skills for getting into more mischief before they get sent to prison as adults."

"Why was it your only school psychology job?"

"I liked the idea of having the credentials to work with kids, but the institutional aspect of the profession and the testing and identifying kids to fit into arbitrary categories didn't set with me."

"It took you away from your beloved rodeo is what you really mean."

"It didn't take me away so much as it interfered. Priorities, you know." He grinned, but his smile faded, and he drifted to a private place in his memories. Coming back to himself, he said, "Roger said you're a writer and librarian."

"Roger again?"

He gave her a half grin. "I had to find out about you some way."

"I have a Bachelors and a Masters in library science from Kent State University. I'm a research librarian."

"Interesting work. Do you have an area of specialization?"

"Yes. World War II. I'm fluent in German, which is part of the reason I gravitated toward that period in history. Being able to read documents and books written in German has opened up a host of additional research I wouldn't have access to otherwise."

Owen nodded. "Fluent. That's impressive. I'm functional in Spanish." He grinned. "Mostly cuss words."

Janae giggled. "I began learning German in kindergarten."

"How did you get from Ohio to Colorado?"

"My first job was with Midwest Library Association in acquisitions as a reviewer of scholarly books for their monthly journal. They purchased the Rocky Mountains Public Library System and moved the main office here. Since I was the newest employee, and there was massive reorganization resulting in cutting or combining positions, I had to find a new job or move to Denver and keep my seniority and benefits."

"Logical reason to move."

"On the upside, I received a substantial bonus and a moving stipend, which made the move even more attractive. It also appealed to me to be able to work mostly from home, since reading, researching, and writing aren't job responsibilities that require my fulltime, physical presence at the library."

"What do you do the two-and-a-half days you go to the library?"

"Research, mostly, and I meet with my supervisor. We discuss potential books for me to read and review. Sometimes she gets special review requests and passes those on to me. Recently, she's expanded my assigned genres to include select fiction. I'm enjoying that very much."

"Is writing reviews what Roger meant when he said you're a writer?"

"Probably. I doubt he knows I've written my first novel, although I haven't had it proofread and edited yet. I'll submit it for publication someday."

"I'm impressed. Educated, independent, and pretty."

She warmed all over at his compliment.

"What's your novel about?"

"An American female photojournalist during World War II masquerading as a man makes it to the front lines of several battles."

"Sounds adventurous." The phone rang. He excused himself. "Hello, Mom. Yeah, after she drops Tony at the airport, she'll come here and give me a ride to rehab." He listened, made briefs comments, listened some more. "You're welcome. It's about time you and Dad got away from the ranch. Enjoy the trip."

Janae went to the couch, kicked off her flip-flops, tucked her legs up under her skirt, and half reclined on a pillow propped against the couch arm.

Owen smiled at something his mom said. "Yeah. Laurel told me about the microburst." He alternately listened and responded. "Doc Harris made me swear I'd stay in Denver until he releases me. He knows what I'll do if I go home too soon." His grin widened. "Of course, I promised to follow doctor's orders. I want my medical release and my driver's license back by New Year's and, if I piss him off, he'll postpone it out of sheer cussedness." He listened and occasionally chuckled or grunted or gave one-word responses.

"No. That's not it. The hold-up on the license is the reaction time to move my right foot from accelerator to brake and vice versa. Clutching with my left isn't a problem. Using my left foot on the brake isn't, either, if it's an automatic." He listened again. "Yeah. The reality is I may not be able to drive a stick anymore, or at least not for the foreseeable future. We'll see. I'll ask Doc if I can start pushing my tolerance of riding in a vehicle." He nodded. "Yes. I know someone here who will drive me."

A long silence and nodding on Owen's part ensued. "Yes. Laurel made me promise I wouldn't back out if Doc says I can travel that far. No." He laughed. "My fingers weren't crossed. If he okays it, I promise I won't stay here by myself, and I'll let someone be my chauffeur. Love you, too. Tell Dad I said *hi*. Don't worry about anything at the ranch while you're gone. Take lots of pictures. Love you, too. Bye."

"That sounded like your parents are going on a trip."

"And both sets of grandparents. Whole family chipped in."

"Oh. That's nice. Where?"

"They're making a pilgrimage of sorts to our Quinlan and O'Leary ancestral locations in the United Kingdom. They'll tour the Orkney Islands and ferry across the English Channel to Calais and Dunkirk, and any other side trips they can work in. They leave Saturday morning. My sisters and a couple of cousins took care of the details, which suited everyone else. Me, in particular." Owen grinned at some private thought.

"I saw pictures of your family's ranch in a hundredth anniversary magazine article. Your ranch is huge and beautiful in a stark and barren, treeless sort of way."

"Typical northeastern Colorado prairie."

"The article explained about your family's business, although I didn't understand much of it. I know next to nothing about rodeo and even less about stock contracting. I do recall the ranch has been in your family since 1897."

"That's right. Twin daughters of the couple who owned the land married cowboy brothers who were among the forerunners of rodeo in Colorado. We laugh about rodeo being a mutated gene on both sides of the family, and it's been passed down through the generations. I can probably name on one hand the family members who aren't involved in rodeo in some way. We specialize in bulls."

"I recall reading that on your family's business website."

"My sister Dana handles the marketing, and she takes care of my website and the business website. I write up my articles, and she takes it from there. My sister Ashley and my two grandmas handle the books. My mom's got her fingers in everything behind the scenes." Owen put the phone on the charger base. "I'm sorry I hit you."

"I shouldn't have barged in and sneaked up on you."

"Does it help that I've wanted a reason to get to know you? With my broken back, meeting women hasn't been at the top of my to-do list, and you keep to yourself so much, the opportunity didn't offer itself."

"Really? You've wanted to meet me? On purpose? Even after what you said on the pho— I mean even after that day you dropped your mail, and I...I..." Blushing warmed her cheeks.

"Stared at my crotch?" Owen grinned. "I didn't mind."

Janae grimaced. "That was so awful of me."

"I figured that's why you went to such lengths to avoid me from then on."

"It was." She hesitated. "Owen, I have to clarify something to keep from causing myself further embarrassment and to appease my conscience."

"Sounds serious."

"First, I'm not a home-wrecker. Second, rebound relationships never work out. They're invariably based on sex, which is a shaky foundation at best and results in hard feelings for both parties when it ends."

Chapter Five

"What are you talking about?"

"What I heard you say on the phone."

"To my mom?"

"No. The other call. Laurel and your boys." There. She'd said it.

Owen stared at her. When her meaning hit him, he laughed too long and too hard, which sent the needle on her humiliation meter spiking into the red zone. She slipped on her flip-flops and left the couch under the impetus of her coping strategy of choice—avoidance.

"Owen. I have to go. I've overstayed as it is."

"No. Please, don't leave. I'm sorry." He held his hands out in apology. "It just struck me funny. Laurel is the youngest of my three sisters. I'm in partnership with her husband, Tony Mathers, Dana's husband, Shawn Robards, and Ashley's husband, Gabe Castillo. The four of us have a training program for rodeo clowns and bullfighters. We take 15 to 20 applicants every three months for a ten-day program. It's intense train-ing."

"Laurel...is your sister? Not the mother of your children? Not your wife? Or ex-wife?"

"Nope. I've never been married. I don't have any kids. And, not that you asked, but you're thinking it, I'm not seeing anyone, either."

Janae sat back. "I suppose I deserved that. I shouldn't have assumed what I did from hearing a one-sided conversation."

"No harm done. Now that we have my bachelor status es-tablished, what about you? Roger and I haven't noticed any men coming to call."

"Are you sure you and Roger aren't secretly dating for as close as you seem to be?"

Owen laughed. "I'll pass that on to his fiancée, Margo."

"Is that her name? She seems lovely. Didn't she just recently move in with him?"

"Yeah. Last weekend. So...are you?"

"Am I what?"

"Seeing someone?"

Janae hesitated, then shrugged. "Library work, book re-viewing, and writing keeps me busy."

"I hear something unsaid in those excuses. Maybe I shouldn't have assumed you date men."

"What? I like men. I'm not— I don't like women. I mean, I like women just fine."

His too-pleased-with-himself grin aggravated her.

"That was mean."

"Yeah, but it was funny, and you're easy to tease."

"To answer your question, I'm not seeing anyone. And may I say there is a fine line between teasing and boorish?"

"Point taken. I'll hold off on teasing until we get to know each other better. Deal?"

"That's a left-handed apology if I ever heard one, but I tentatively accept."

"Good. What can I get you to drink besides water? Pop?"

"Nothing alcoholic."

"I'm putting on fresh coffee."

Janae made a face.

"I'll take that as you don't drink coffee."

"I don't. Hot tea with honey would be wonderful."

"No doubt herbal."

"Naturally."

Owen grunted and shook his head. "You stay cozy right there on the couch. I'll see what I can come up with. My mom stashed chicken noodle soup, saltines, and tea in the cabinet in case I came down with a cold or the flu." Taking up the bottle of bourbon and the two whiskey glasses, he went to the kitchen.

Janae settled against the couch pillow, a satisfied smile playing at her lips.

He's not married.

While Owen took care of the left-over pizza, Janae went to the bathroom, sorely wishing for her toothbrush to get rid of the after-pizza taste and settling for a swig of mouthwash and scrubbing her teeth with her finger. Inspecting her face again, she was dismayed to find the mark across the bridge of her nose darkening and spreading. Surely, the puffiness around her eyes wasn't already from the swelling. She was overtired, that's all.

The reality of being in Owen's apartment sank in. They'd had supper and conversation and laughs. He was friendly and hospitable and, more importantly, he seemed interested in her.

Self-doubt instantly surfaced. How could that be? She wasn't a head-turner. She was a reclusive librarian whose life consisted of research and writing.

Tingling sensations around her mouth and across her cheeks warned of an impending panic attack, but it hit her so fast she didn't have time to talk herself out of it with deep breathing and positive self-talk. The next thing she knew, she was sitting on the hallway floor with Owen kneeling beside her.

"Bout of vertigo?"

She nodded. "Anxiety. Panic attack." The words were breathy.

"Have I made you that uncomfortable? I really don't go around punching women. In fact, you're the first, and I'm feeling pretty low about it."

He checked her pupils and pulse.

Janae managed a little smile. "It's not you. It's me. Socializing is not my strength."

"Social phobia is rough. Add that to getting your glasses smashed against your face, I don't think it's a good idea for you to be alone tonight. Do you have anyone who can stay with you? Co-worker? Someone here in the building?"

"I haven't made those kinds of acquaintances."

"Then you'll stay here. I'll be up painting. You can have my bed or stay on the couch. I've spent many a night out here. As far as couches go, it's decent for sleeping."

She caught her breath. Owen Quinlan had invited her to stay the night. Granted, it wasn't a romantic liaison, but it was more than she'd ever dreamed would happen. Funny how she was grateful for a panic attack.

"I'll take the couch, if you don't mind. I'd like to watch you paint."

"I don't mind at all. Having company will be a nice change."

Owen helped her to the couch, brought her a bed pillow and the afghan, and tucked her in. In a few minutes, her own late nights of reading and writing caught up with her, and drowsiness prevailed over her efforts to stay awake. She went to sleep breathing in the soothing, subtle hint of Owen's aftershave that lingered on the pillow.

When next she opened her eyes, it took her several moments to identify her unfamiliar surroundings. The smell of warm, moist air of a shower brought her back to where she was. In another few seconds, Owen, barefoot, wearing sweat pants and tugging on a t-shirt, walked toward her from the hallway.

"I was just going to wake you. How're you feeling?"

"Headachy. What time is it?"

"One thirty. Here." He indicated the glass of water and bottle of acetaminophen on the coffee table. "Roger brought it up."

Aghast, Janae sat up. "You didn't tell him I was here, did you?"

"I was tempted, but no." He grinned, shook out two tablets, then handed them and the water to her.

"Thank you."

"You're welcome. I'm going to bed. Are you okay out here?"

Janae snuggled down under the afghan. "Yes."

"All right. Wake me if you need anything. I'm an early riser. I'll be quiet when I get up so you can sleep."

"Oh. Don't worry about me. Normally, I'd go to the library in the morning, but the schedule changed this week. I'm working at home instead."

"Goodnight."

"Goodnight."

Janae made her way to the bathroom, muttering to herself that it was entirely too early to be up after such an eventful night.

"Breakfast is ready. Coffee's on. Tea's steeping," Owen called from the kitchen.

"Be right there," she grumbled. Her reflection in the mirror did nothing to lift her mood. She did what she could to freshen herself and smooth out her hair then she went to the kitchen.

"Good morning." Owen's grin worked its way into a smile. "Nice shiners."

"Don't you dare laugh." Janae squinted a frown at him.

"There's nothing you can do about it, so you'd just as well laugh."

"I wasn't expecting the bruising and swelling to be this pronounced." She sat at the four-chair, drop-leaf table.

Owen brought the tea kettle to the table and put it on a hot pad beside the cup and matching saucer then went back to the counter. Janae filled her cup, stirred in a spoonful of honey, then held the cup to her face to feel the steamy warmth and inhale the pleasant aroma.

Owen returned to the table with a plate of bagels fresh from the toaster and placed them beside the cream cheese and bowl of sliced strawberries. He poured coffee for himself and sat across from her. "You're going to get lots of attention from people wondering how you got two black eyes."

"Even my forehead is bruised. How long will I look like this?"

"The colors will steadily change and fade. You won't notice it in two or three weeks."

"Three weeks?"

He chuckled at her distress. "Haven't you ever barked your shins? It takes a while for the color to go away."

"Barked my shins? I've never heard that expression. And no, I've never had a bruise like this. The worst I've ever been hurt was a bloody lip and skinned knees when I learned to ride a bike."

"Seriously? How have you managed to get through life so unscathed?"

Janae sighed and shrugged. "It's complicated and not at all interesting." She spread cream cheese on a bagel, topped it with strawberries, took a bite, and then a sip of tea.

"Are you going to explain or just leave me hanging?"

"Oh... I'm sorry. I thought we were just making breakfast talk. Well, I suppose— No. It would bore you."

"Tell me anyway. I like uninteresting, complicated stories."

She made a face at him. "You're hilarious."

"Thanks. I think so, too." He grinned.

She took a sip of tea, thought about it, and said, "I wouldn't know where to start."

Chapter Six

Owen encouraged her. "Start anywhere. You can always jump back and forth and fill in things as you remember them."

"All right. Well, I'm an only child. My mother miscarried numerous times and only carried two babies to near-full term, and then under intense medical care. One of those two babies was stillborn. I was their last hope. I was sickly for years."

"Sickly, how?"

"Asthma, weak lungs, allergies, although I grew up to be quite healthy. I so badly wanted a pet, specifically a cat, but my mother said they were dirty creatures, and I'd no doubt be allergic. Most social gatherings were considered risky because of communal germs, although I was vaccinated for every disease known to man."

She rolled her eyes. Owen laughed outright.

"I took piano lessons three times a week, which I enjoyed. I won several recital awards." She sighed. "I miss having a piano." She sipped tea before she continued. "I was so gangly and clumsy that my parents thought ballet lessons would improve my coordination. It didn't. I thought bowling would be fun, but it wasn't clean enough to suit my mother. I did play badminton competitively in junior high and high school, which I enjoyed.

"Outside of the failed ballet experiment, my social interactions were carefully orchestrated. Since my parents believed other people's children were potentially bad influences, only two girls were allowed to spend the night, and that was because my parents approved of their families more than any of the others. I was never allowed to stay over with them, though,"

"Makes me sad for you."

"I did get to spend as much time as I wanted with both sets of grandparents. That part of my growing up was wonderful. My parents monitored everything I did to the point that sometimes it felt like I was smothering, but I was such a sensitive child that it physically hurt me if I thought I'd disappointed them in any way. My mother is the queen of manipulation."

"First off, that's an unhealthy way to raise kids. Second, it goes hand in hand with attending private school."

"I won't disagree, and yes. I never attended a public school. Kindergarten through eighth grade was an all-girls school. High school was co-ed. They were expensive schools and selective about the families accepted. I've probably made it sound like my childhood was a nightmare. It wasn't. I had freedom within strict limits." Janae tossed her head to shake off the gray clouds of those memories. "In their defense, my parents aren't ogres. They're good people."

"You don't have to apologize. Dealing with family isn't always easy. What about extended family. Do you have cousins? Aunts and uncles?"

"Yes, but I haven't kept in touch as well as I should have since college. There's a family reunion scheduled next summer.

I haven't decided whether I'll go. I suppose I should." She shrugged that she really didn't want to.

"What do your parents do for a living?"

"My dad and mom are tax accountants."

"Grandparents?"

"My mom's parents, Rainsford and Amelia Brock, were college professors until they retired. My paternal grandparents are Andrew and Evelyn. Everyone calls them Andy and Evie. They owned a realty business that they sold a few years ago. Now that they're retired, they keep themselves busy with volunteer work. They get their names and photographs in the paper with some regularity for their fundraising event of the month or the social issue they're lobbying for or against."

Owen smiled. "What did you do for fun when you were growing up? How did you not go stir crazy?"

"We vacationed every year someplace new. That was fun. I had my books and writing and a well-developed imagination. Once I reached high school, my parents allowed me more personal freedom. I could go to the movie with friends—in groups and matinees only, mind you." Janae shrugged. "I was a stagehand in theater class. I sang in the school choir, and I continued piano lessons until I graduated high school."

"That's a lot more like a normal childhood."

"Yes. We spent a summer in Germany with my air force colonel uncle when I was fourteen. That was a lot of fun, especially being able to speak German. Things like that."

"Didn't you ever rebel?"

"Oh, no."

"Not even a little?"

"Oh, I managed little victories in small, passive-aggressive ways, none of which are worth mentioning nor am I particularly proud of doing them."

"All kids do that. It's called testing the limits. You're saying you never rocked the parent boat? Never got yourself grounded for ignoring curfew? Didn't dye your hair green on St. Paddy's Day? Get a tattoo at the mall, or pierce your ears?"

Janae giggled. "No."

"Really? I'm skeptical."

Janae wrinkled her nose and glanced sideways at him. "Well, there was that one thing in high school. Well, more than once, one thing. It was something I was in complete control of that they weren't. It was the first secret I kept from them, and the first real risk I'd ever taken. Even then, I took all the necessary precautions."

"All...the...necessary...precautions. I'd hazard a guess it's one of two scenarios. You got drunk and stayed at a friend's house to sober up, or you slept with someone."

"Are you speaking from your own teenage experiences?"

Owen grinned. "Let's just say I was grounded a lot."

Janae smiled. "I don't doubt it."

"So, which was it? Alcohol or sex...or a combination of both?"

"Not alcohol."

"Okay. Process of elimination. You slept with the high school quarterback."

Janae scoffed. "Of course not. The captain of the chess team."

"Of course, he was." Owen chuckled. "That's a pretty significant risk for high school kids."

"Yes, it was, although we were seniors and both eighteen."

"And that's it?"

"Yes."

"What about in college?"

"I was very dedicated to my studies."

"So, no frat parties or panty raids?"

"Certainly not, especially since there was no thought of attending any college but Kent State with my grandparents being professors there, and it being my dad's alma mater. Plus, it's right down the street from where I grew up.

"I didn't live in a dorm, and I didn't move out on my own until I was in the first year of my master's program." She let Owen do the math.

Owen lifted an eyebrow. "That was... What? Five, six years after high school?"

Cringing, Janae said, "I know. I know."

"What made you move out?"

"Two fellow grad students who needed a third roommate to share expenses invited me to live with them. It wasn't as awful as I'd anticipated when I told my parents."

"That was an independent step in the right direction."

"It was until the female roommate moved out to live with her boyfriend. That left the male roommate and me. Alone. Cohabitating. We went from roommates to more than roommates, and we didn't look for a third person to share expenses. My parents were deeply disappointed in me."

"Ah. The obligatory, and hypocritical, generational social stigma of living together out of wedlock." Owen washed down a bite of bagel with a gulp of coffee. "I'm shocked, I tell you, shocked, at your wanton rebellion. As an adult. Living your own life. Making your own decisions. Paying your own way. Traveling your own road."

Janae laughed until her sides hurt at his histrionic pseudo-outrage.

Chapter Seven

"They tolerated my living arrangement. Grudgingly. When they discovered he was from a respected, money-eyed family from Pennsylvania, he became a *good catch* and our unmarried cohabitation ceased to be as much of a problem. They were soon to be disappointed again when we broke up a few months later. He received a fellowship to study abroad. We split as friends." She looked over the cup at Owen. "I haven't missed him."

"Maybe once your parents approved, you lost interest in using him as your weapon of independence."

"*Hmm.* Weapon of independence. That is an interesting concept." Janae nodded lightly. "No. I think the underlying problem was I didn't love him. Just like I didn't love my high school boyfriend."

"That'll do it, all right."

"Speaking from experience?"

Owen lifted a shoulder in *maybe*. He changed the subject. "So, moving out here was metaphorically cutting the apron strings."

"I suppose. That, and a great opportunity. Don't get me wrong, I love my parents, and I don't regret my childhood, but the longer I've been here, the more of a relief it's been to be away from them. I feel guilty about that, sometimes. Well, more than sometimes. Okay, often. I'm so not looking forward to going home for Thanksgiving."

"When did you move to Denver?"

"Memorial Day weekend. I house sat for the assistant director of my library, while she spent the summer in London. When she returned, I moved here."

"Must have felt like an adventure to the ends of the earth moving so far from home."

"My father and I flew out. He stayed a week to make sure the moving company delivered my belongings, which I stored where I was house-sitting. He helped me buy a car. As it turned out, I was glad I hadn't gotten a driver's license before I moved. It wasn't nearly as involved as I'd anticipated."

"Wait. The way you said that sounded like you just got your license. Like for the first time."

"That's right."

Owen considered that. "Taken together, all those are accomplishments toward independence. That's gotta make you feel good."

"It does."

"Why are you dreading Thanksgiving?"

"Because I know my parents. They'll make me feel guilty for liking it here. My mother more than my father. She assures me the newness will wear off. They don't believe I'm happy no matter what I say."

Owen nodded thoughtfully. "So, you're afraid you'll abandon your independence to keep their approval for fear of losing their love if you don't."

Janae put her cup down. "That's quite a theory. Must you armchair analyze everything I say?"

"Refute me."

"I will. It's obligation. They've given me so much. If something had happened to me, it would have devastated them. It still will. I don't like worrying them. My childhood was happy in its overly sheltered way. I felt loved and safe."

"It seems to me you're doing exactly what you need to do for yourself. You're leading your own life, making your own way. They know you have to. You know you have to. Your relationship with them will be the better for it."

"I hope so. One thing I know for sure is I'm never having children."

"Where did that come from?"

"Thinking about my childhood."

"Never is a bold absolute. Why not?"

"Many reasons, not the least of which is why it is assumed just because I'm female that I automatically want to be a mother? I've never held a baby. I wouldn't have the slightest idea what to do. My life revolves around reading, research, and writing. The thought of baseball practices or dance lessons and school activities—" She shuddered. "I can't picture myself doing any of those. Plus, there's such constant worry that something will happen to your child. It's simply too much responsibility. I watched the effects that worry had on my parents."

"Your parents are not the norm." Owen refilled his coffee cup then leaned against the counter looking at her.

"You're looking at me with an odd expression that I don't really care for."

"*The lady doth protest too much, methinks.*"

"Are you insinuating that I'm insincere? That I don't know my own feelings?"

"Could be it's your subconscious resentment of being smother-mothered during your childhood. That resentment has manifested as your payback to your parents by being turned off of marriage and motherhood."

Janae bristled. "I am under no obligation to produce children for my parents' enjoyment, fulfillment, or satisfaction or for anyone else's."

"I agree completely. Women aren't baby incubators despite the drivel those wacko groups spout. But you brought it up. I'm just commenting. That aside, Janae, every parent is a first-time parent. It's a learn-as-you-experience situation. Every parent worries about their kids. It's in the rule book for raising them."

"Oh, really. Do children have a rule book, too?"

"No. They make everything up as they go. They turn their parents' lives inside out and upside down with sleepless nights, heartache, frustration, and challenges in exchange for laughter, kisses, hugs, first smile, first step, first word, the first...everything. It's amazing to watch a child learn and see their world opening up."

"And you're making these bold statements from firsthand experience? You said you don't have children."

"I have nieces and nephews."

Janae granted him that.

"It's not the kid's job to make parenting easy, but it is the parents' job to be the best parents they can be, so that little girl or boy can grow into the adult who can be the best parent they can be. It's a circle of life thing."

"For the sake of discussion, I won't disagree, but what you've described is the ideal situation where there are two parents who share the same familial values and goals. Speaking for myself, I don't see marriage or long-term commitment for that matter in my future, therefore, motherhood is not for me, and I certainly have no aspirations to be a single parent."

"What do you want?"

"My doctorate, although I'm undecided on the focus, and I want to be a published author of some financial success."

"Those are great goals, as long as you don't look back in regret that you limited yourself on experiencing the other things life has to offer. Those are socially isolating goals. It's hard for me to believe that you don't want someone in your life to share the journey to your doctorate as well as be a part of your publishing aspirations."

Owen walked to her.

"People don't regret not having a bigger house or fancier car or not taking that vacation to some outrageously over-priced amusement park. They regret not saying *I love you* more often to the people who matter to them. They regret not showing more kindness and compassion. They regret not watching sunsets and looking at full moons with someone they love. They wish they'd walked hand in hand on a snowy winter night just to do it. They regret the risks they didn't take."

"Do you have risk-regret?"

"No. There are things I want in my life that haven't happened yet, but not because I'm afraid to go after them. The time isn't right."

"Such as?"

"I'm going to open a camp—I don't know what to call it yet—for troubled and disadvantaged kids."

"You mean a rodeo camp?"

"That's too narrow. I want to offer kids a broader experience. A ranch camp or a country adventure."

"Have you considered you'll have to stop tempting death in a rodeo arena to live long enough to create that camp? Can you really leave that part of your life behind?"

Owen didn't say anything for a few moments. "I don't know. I'll face that when I have to, and I don't have to right now."

"What do you want in your personal life?"

"Me? That's easy. I'm an old-fashioned guy."

"That tells me nothing. Tell me something *personal*."

"Like what?"

"All guys have issues. Baggage of lost love. Jilted at the altar and left to die slowly of a broken heart."

"That sounds like the plot to the romance novels my sisters devour. I'm just me. My childhood was great. I've loved and lost, and I've gone on. I'll keep on keeping on."

"Meaning Ms. Right will eventually come riding along on her white horse and sweep you off your feet?"

Owen chuckled. "Interesting mental image."

"That romantic scenario might be a problem where you're concerned, because I maintain you have a death wish, which is a huge issue."

"Maybe if I wasn't trained in what I do, I might—*might*—agree with you, but what I do is an art. And I'm damn good." He topped off his coffee then studied her for a few moments.

"Janae, rodeo is my life. It's not baggage. There are no deep-rooted psychological issues attached to it. You opened the baggage you've been lugging around all these years for me to see. I appreciate that. What I saw there is you've learned to be afraid of your shadow and of disappointing your parents. Your parents probably didn't intend to do that, but it's how it affected you. It made you afraid of life. You're afraid to make wrong decisions.

"When you finally do make a decision or a choice, you still agonize over whether it was the right one. I'm not talking about the everyday things we all deal with. I mean the big ones. The life-impacting ones. Relationships. Independence. Employment. You need to give yourself permission to reset your perspective. Change your perspective, and you change your reality. You know...find out what condition your condition is in."

She recognized the self-amused grin tugging his mustache as entertaining himself with an inside joke that had gone over her head. What she wasn't sure of was if he was making fun of her or being serious.

Frowning, and a little put out, she said, "I'm not saying I agree or disagree. I have to think about this."

Chapter Eight

Owen asked, "Could you have taken a different job and stayed in Kent?"

"Yes."

"Did you agonize over the decision?"

"I was practically sick over it."

"The important thing is you followed through on something you wanted for yourself. Maybe part of that decision was a subconscious way to escape from the emotional trap you've been in all your life."

"You make it sound as if I ran away from home."

"In a manner of speaking, you did. Are you homesick?"

She considered it. "I miss my family and a really close friend."

"That's not the same thing. Are you sorry you left?"

"Sometimes."

"But you don't want to go back. Why?"

"I love my job."

"Only your job?"

Exasperated at his persistence, she said, "All right. So, I love the freedom of having my own apartment in a city too far for my parents to drop in at their whim."

Owen smiled, seemingly satisfied at her response. "You've gotten a taste of freedom, and you don't want to lose it. Run with it. Don't hide out in this apartment and watch the world through the window as it passes by. Get out there and be a participant."

"That is too close to hedonism, which is rife with selfishness and irresponsibility."

Owen chuckled. "All right. Don't take it that far. All I'm saying is life shovels out enough heartache and puts obstacles in our way on its own without us deliberately adding more. We have to look for, and hang onto, the joys that come our way—and go on the adventures that make life worth living. If we don't, what's the point of getting out of bed every morning? It's impossible to control every aspect of our lives. Why try? All we can do is make the best decisions we can with the best information we have, and then let everything else take care of itself."

"You're assuming I'm not living life exactly the way I want. I like order and serenity. I like things to be predictable and planned. I'm not adventurous, and I have no aspirations to change that. Living life through stories in books that I read recreationally is exciting enough for me. It's safe."

His mustache twitched with his smug smile. "Keep telling yourself that, and maybe you'll eventually believe it."

Janae scowled. "You're mocking me."

"Guilty."

Janae folded her napkin with meticulous care, buying time to squash the anger bubbling up. Shoulders set, she crossed the tiled floor with purpose, and stopped in front of Owen. She glanced at the wall clock.

"Thirteen hours ago, a conceited, egotistical, know-it-all cowboy punched me in the nose, blackened my eyes, broke my glasses, and proceeded to criticize everything about my life he deems needs correcting according to his man-ego, which is wildly inflated."

"Don't forget, he plied you with whiskey, bought you dinner, and invited you to spend the night with him." He wiggled his eyebrows.

The smirk wrapped around his innuendo infuriated her. She buried her fist in his mid-section, doubling him over. His cup spewed coffee when it hit the floor. Stomping into the living room, Janae snatched up her key lanyard and headed for the door.

Half-crouched, holding his stomach and trying to catch his breath and laugh at the same time, Owen caught up with her as she yanked the door open. The coat rack toppled, wedged across the doorframe, and everything hanging on it further hampered her exit.

"Wait. Janae, I'm sorry."

"I don't believe you." She wiped tears as she attempted to right the coat rack, only to send it crashing the other way, but now Owen was in the doorway blocking her exodus. Exasperated, with more tears threatening, she leveled a glare on Owen. "Please move aside."

"Really. I'm sorry. Sometimes I don't know when to stop. I was always pissing off my sisters when we were kids. Well... I still do. They constantly tell me my charming personality...isn't. Like now."

"You're right. You're not charming. You're an ass."

"I'll give you that. Please, don't leave angry. Talk to me."

"What should I say?" Janae met his eyes squarely, her body trembling with her aversion to confrontation, but furious enough to stand up for herself. "That you don't—or won't—understand that not everyone wants what you want out of life? We've known each other for half a day, and you're presuming that I want your opinion of how I'm living my life.

"You are wildly egotistical. You and I are cut from two entirely different bolts of cloth. You need to respect that I don't look at life the way you do, and I don't have to. In fact, I don't want to be like you. I can't relate to your *seize everything life throws at you and never flinch* philosophy."

She threw her hands in the air, exasperated.

"Furthermore, I'm not a violent person, and I let you make me so angry that I hit you. You aren't good for me. In fact, you bring out the worst in me."

"I don't go around hitting people, either." He grinned. "We're even now."

"That's not funny. Please move."

He didn't vacate his position. "Wait... Janae... I admit I overstepped. I'm sorry. There's nothing that can't be solved with a good laugh, a long talk over a bottle of wine, and a rowdy romp in bed."

"You are the most vexing person I've ever known. How did we go from you hurting my feelings and making fun of me to redirecting this as something sexual?"

He grinned. "Freudian slip. Forgive me?"

"No. You need to stop analyzing me. It annoys me, and it's beyond arrogant on your part."

He shrugged. "It's in my nature."

"That's an excuse for being an obnoxious jerk and not taking responsibility for how your words and superior attitude hurts others."

"My sisters would agree with you."

"Then maybe you're the one who needs therapy to learn better interpersonal skills and consideration for someone other than yourself. Do you analyze men, or is it just women?"

Owen's grin froze then slowly faded and realization showed in its place.

"That's what I thought. You're a misogynistic lout. I don't think I like you."

Owen squinted, shaking his head. "No. Not misogynistic. Not even a hint. I'm sorry I came across like that."

"What would you call it?"

"Unrestrained ego that needed to be brought down several notches, which you've done. I'm sorry. Really."

"You're too self-absorbed to be sorry."

"Give me a chance to show you that I'm sincere."

"How will you do that?"

"Do you have plans tonight?"

"That's none of your business."

He worked his jaw around keeping a smile from showing. "If you decide you don't have plans, come back at six. I'll have something properly healthy for supper to make up for last night's artery-clogging pizza."

"An apology supper?"

"I'd like to think of it as another opportunity to get to know each other supper."

"You haven't offered enough redeeming qualities for me to want to know you better."

"Ooh. Low blow. I probably deserved that."

"Probably?"

"All right. I deserved it. What about supper?"

"Dinner dates are best kept for weekends. I have job responsibilities during the week."

"We'll keep it short."

Still, she hesitated.

"Please."

"I'll think about it."

"Any food allergies other than M-S-G? Foods you absolutely won't eat?"

She lost her internal battle between wanting to make her point by not accepting his supper invitation, and that she really did want to get to know him better. "I'm allergic to fish. I've always been a picky eater, but I'm willing to try a food once. Oh. Not raspberries. I detest the flavor."

"I won't get crazy with the menu." He cocked an ear toward voices. "Just as well stick around. Sounds like Laurel and the boys are on the way up. I'll introduce you."

Janae sucked in a gasp. "Oh no! They can't see me like this. I have to go."

"Too late." Owen stepped into the hallway to let her pass.

"Uncle Owen!" The boys waved and ran ahead.

Janae turned her head in an attempt to shield her face from Laurel's scrutiny even though she muttered a polite *good morning* when they met and passed.

"Owen, did I see that woman come from your apartment? She looked a little roughed up."

Janae glanced back to see Laurel slap her hands on her hips, clearly disapproving.

"She spent the night with you, didn't she? Owen Patrick Quinlan, what kind of bedroom games do you play? Did you black her eyes?"

Janae hurried to the end of the hallway and the looming sanctuary of the stairway.

"Laurel, you know me better than that. I've never lifted a hand to a woman, but I will remind you I broke my back. I wasn't castrated."

Janae gasped and whirled, caught her feet in her skirt, and sent her flip-flops flying down the stairs. She stumbled after them, hot embarrassment coursing through her body with Owen's laughter chasing her to the second floor.

She hoped he choked.

Chapter Nine

Butterflies the size of pterodactyls took flight in her stomach. Plain-Jane Janae, as she was taunted in school, was going to Owen Quinlan's apartment for an actual dinner date. Her irritation with him wasn't gone, but it had become manageable after a few hours of self-reflection to admit that much of what he'd said was true.

She stood before her full-length mirror, checking and rechecking her appearance. Thank heavens for contact lenses. Her glasses didn't come close to fitting over the swelling. She'd changed her clothes three times before coming back to the first outfit—a lavender maxi skirt with a coordinating three-quarter sleeve tunic of lavender and green flowers against white with new, slip-on canvas sneakers.

Looking at her reflection, she went into her practiced self-talk for situations where she felt completely uncomfortable, but still had to get through them.

"What am I doing? All he did was make fun of me and make me mad. Don't read too much into this. It's just supper." She waggled her finger at her reflection. "Stop it. If he didn't want to see me again, he wouldn't go to all the work to cook supper for me." She whooshed out a breath to bolster her nerves. She wasn't sure she believed herself.

Precisely at six, Janae knocked on Owen's door.

"It's open." His voice was muffled from well within the apartment.

She entered, closed the door, and lingered, listening to the music until she identified it as Brahms' Violin Concerto in D major. The apartment looked the same except for the tray of crackers and cheese, two long stem wine glasses, and a bottle of white wine chilling in an ice bucket on the coffee table.

Owen walked from his bedroom. "Glad to see you. Your outfit is pretty. The colors complement your black eyes and really bring out the purple." He grinned wider with every step.

"Do you never stop teasing?"

"Nope. Wine?" He indicated the coffee table. "Sauvignon Blanc."

"Yes, please."

"I took a chance that you don't have an aversion to all alcohol."

"You guessed correctly. I like wine."

"Take your pick. Couch or chair."

She sat on the couch, Owen poured wine, then he sat in the chair.

"How's your face? Headache?"

"No headache. Just swollen and tender."

"Did you get your review finished on time?"

"Yes. I send them by email."

He nodded. "That's convenient."

"Yes, it is."

"Do you like the wine?"

"Very much. Excellent choice. I love the grapefruity tartness in Sauvignon Blanc."

"I do, too."

"Um... I don't mean to be critical, but I don't smell food. Did I misunderstand your invitation was for supper?"

"No. You understood right. You don't smell food, because there isn't any."

"But you said you'd cook supper."

"No. I said I'd provide supper. I didn't say I'd cook it."

"I don't—"

The knock on the door interrupted her.

"Supper's here." Owen put his wine glass on the coffee table and went to the door. "Right on time."

Owen opened the door and greeted the two people carrying to-go boxes labeled *The Denver Grill*. "Kitchen's through there." He pointed. "Put 'em on the counter. We'll take it from there."

"Here's your credit card receipt."

"And here's a tip."

"Thank you. Call us again."

"I will."

Owen closed the door behind them and returned to Janae. Slightly bowing and indicating the kitchen, he said, "Supper's ready, *milady*."

Janae giggled. "Thank you, kind sir." She accepted his hand.

"It smells good. *The Denver Grill* is on the way to the library. I've wondered about the quality of the food."

"I've never been disappointed, and I order from them a couple times a month."

Janae removed the foil from each of the disposable containers. "Chicken alfredo. Caesar salad. Ooh. Garlic mashed potatoes. I can smell the garlic." She leaned close to the bread and breathed in the aroma. "*Mmm*. Rosemary. I have a weakness for bread. I have to watch myself in that regard."

"And here's dessert." Owen opened the box.

"Angel food cake. My favorite."

"Mine, too. Orange sherbet's in the freezer."

"Orange sherbet? With the cake?"

"You can't beat it. Let it melt just a little, and it's better than strawberries and whipped cream."

"I've never had angel food cake and orange sherbet. I would never have thought they'd go together."

"Fill your plate. Table or living room?"

Janae looked at both. "Table. I'm somewhat of a klutz. I'll be less apt to spill something there."

"Works for me. I'll get the wine."

Janae marveled at how comfortable she felt half-reclining on the couch she'd slept on last night while a man she'd only spoken to in passing slept a room away. That didn't happen in real life, only in romance novels or movies. Still, here she was and there he was, and they were on their second bottle of wine.

"You got quiet all of a sudden. What are you thinking about?"

"I was thinking about how little we know each other in relation to how comfortable I feel right now in a man's apartment drinking wine and talking. We've talked about so many things. Politics and religion and even a few social issues, and we're still speaking to each other."

"That's good, don't you think?"

"I suppose the mannerly thing to do is to invite you to my apartment for supper."

"I am two suppers up on you, unless we call it even Steven for the pizza and the punch with the palette, then I'm only one up."

"Nice alliteration." Janae giggled. "I love that phrase—even Steven. Yes. We are even for last night."

"If you were to invite me to dinner, what does a self-professed picky eater serve a guest who isn't picky?"

"Not much, I can tell you that. I don't like to cook, and I'm not at all good at it when I do cook. I have my usuals that satisfy me."

"What are your usuals?"

"Well, um...for breakfast, I like cereal and milk, muffins, fruit, oatmeal, toast, or a combination of any of it. Oh, and I really like peanut butter toast with sliced bananas."

"I like that, too. What else?"

"Fruit. Cheese. Peanut butter and jam sandwich. Crunchy fresh vegetables. I don't like cooked vegetables other than corn, and I don't like it on the cob. I don't like the way it feels to bite into food with my front teeth. Same with apples. I have to slice them."

"Front teeth, huh?"

"Don't judge."

"I'm not. Sounds like tactile defensiveness."

"That's what I've been told. For supper, I might have broiled chicken or pork, occasionally ham or turkey breast, but not lunchmeat of any kind. I like baked potatoes. Grilled cheese sandwiches and tomato basil soup. I love scalloped potatoes. I have a bit of weakness for dark chocolate."

"Yup. You are sure enough a picky eater. That aside, what would you cook for me?"

Janae shrugged and scrunched her face as much as the soreness allowed. "Nothing. I'd order from *The Denver Grill.*"

Owen laughed. "Fair enough. How about this? Next time we have a supper date, let's cook together."

"That will work, I suppose."

"Yeah. It will." Owen poured himself more wine then held the bottle out. "Some?"

"No, thank you."

Owen sat back in the chair. "I've been thinking that you're dreading going home for Thanksgiving."

"What about it?"

"Can you turn that around and make it a positive experience?"

"What do you mean?"

"If it's spending all your time with your family that you're dreading, then make plans before you get there to minimize your interactions. Come up with an itinerary so you're on the go and not home every minute. Is there a friend you'd like to see? A place you like to hang out? A favorite restaurant? Go to a movie?"

"As a matter of discussion, I will be spending time with my best friend, Gavin. He's a librarian at the university. We met in grad school. He'll finish his Ph.D. next spring. Doctor of Library Science."

"Impressive."

"Yes, it is. I'm so proud of him. Other than my parents and my grandparents, he's the only other person I can say I've ever loved. We laugh that we're each other's free therapy, but it's true. We help each other when we're down or just need to talk, and we celebrate each other's happy times."

"Well, there you are. Sounds like he's your ticket to surviving your trip home. Do you parents like him?"

"Yes."

"Even better. Tell him what you're worried about. Maybe he can be your excuse not to stay home. Ask him to come over and help run interference with your parents." He paused. "Unless that's asking too much for him to arrange his Thanksgiving plans around helping you make yours less stressful."

"Meaning I shouldn't expect others to take care of my problems, because I'm a big girl and should act as such? After all, it's only for Wednesday evening through Sunday morning."

Owen's smile and nod were a little too satisfied. She was going to enjoy turning this back on him.

"You aren't as clever as you think. I know what you did. I asked you to stop analyzing me, so you took a different approach in an attempt to guide me to the right decision."

He simply grinned.

"Well, Mr. Psychologist, you didn't guide me anywhere. I came to that decision when Gavin called this morning. We talked and talked. He was so excited to share his news with me. It made me realize that having people in your life who love you and care about you is more important than coming up with excuses to avoid them. I'm not necessarily looking forward to going home, but it will be just fine. I will be just fine."

Owen lifted his wine glass to her. "Glad to hear it. Out of curiosity, what did Gavin say that changed your mind?"

"He's met someone. The longer Gavin talked about him, the more I realized how selfish I was in considering asking him to be my temporary rescuer, when I have so many things in my life to be grateful for and happy about, my parents and grandparents all being well and healthy being the most important."

"Him? Did you say *him*?"

"Yes. Does that bother you?" She prepared to defend Gavin.

"Not at all. I wanted to make sure I heard right."

"Why?"

"He's your friend. I wouldn't want to insult you through a *faux pas*. Everyone should be allowed to love who they want without society judging or getting in the way."

Janae considered his sincerity and accepted it. "I appreciate that. Well, now. It's your turn."

"For what?"

"Last night, I told you about my personal relationships. It's only fair that you tell me yours. That will put us on equal footing, wouldn't you say?"

"All right." He shrugged. "Not much to say. The few women I've been with were casual to occasional bedroom friends in mutually agreeable no-strings relationships. There was one who could have meant more than that. I was her rebound. Like you said, it's not a foundation to build a lasting relationship on."

"Evidently, long-term commitment isn't our strengths." Janae reached for the wine. Owen beat her to it.

"Let me, and not necessarily."

"Thank you. Not necessarily, what?"

"Commitment. It's a matter of meeting the right person at the right time."

Janae sat back and took a sip from her glass. "What? You're looking at me like there's something on your mind."

He looked at her a moment longer. "Janae, why did you come to my apartment yesterday?"

Chapter Ten

"Your music was too loud."

"You could have called Roger. It's his job. I think something else sent you knocking on my door. Be honest."

"I told you. To ask you to turn your music down."

"I don't believe it."

"Why not?"

"Remember I said you'd never quite passed out?"

"Yeesss." Janae drew the word out suspiciously.

"You talked the entire time. More like muttered. It was entertaining and enlightening."

Janae's heart thumped hard, but she braved the obvious question. "What did I say?"

"You carried on about me removing your black negligee."

Heat blazed up her neck. "You made that up, and I could have been talking about someone else."

His smirk turned to a full smile. "I could have, but I didn't, and you said my name. Repeatedly. You were pretty darn clear on what was happening and who was there and what we were doing. Your fantasies about me brought you to my door, didn't they?"

She hedged. "*Daydreams*. I will only confess to daydreaming about you. Daydreams are harmless diversions. Superficial nothings."

"Call it what you want. What matters is my music was the catalyst that brought us together. I'm glad I annoyed you so much that you acted on your *daydreams*. I'd heard about you and the story was so good, I went out of my way to get a good look at you."

"What do you mean you heard about me? What did you hear?"

"Roger—"

"*Errrg*. Roger."

Owen laughed. "I wasn't here when you set off the emergency stairs alarm. Roger said it was a ring-tailed dog and pony show with the police and fire trucks and everyone evacuating the building."

The heat of embarrassment warmed her cheeks. "Roger promised he'd never reveal that I'm the one who inadvertently caused that. Not even to the emergency responders."

"Your secret is safe. I bribed him."

"You are impossible. In my defense, I didn't do it on purpose. I can read. I know the side stairwells are for fire purposes only. The warnings are clear: *Emergency Exit Only. Do Not Enter. Alarm Will Sound if Door is Opened*. I was walking around, familiarizing myself with the premises and building. When I looked through the stairwell door window on my floor, I evidently rested my hand on the door handle too hard."

"It's a great story. I'm sorry I missed it. Roger wanted to play matchmaker, and I'll confess I was tempted to take him up on his offer, but I decided to leave it alone, what with my back being what it is—and that I'll be out of here around the first of the year."

"Oh... I'm flattered. I thought the same when I first saw you, but putting myself forward to meet people is not in my nature. Just as coming here to confront you about your music was completely out of character. And then talking the way I did..." She cringed. "I'm embarrassed. You have to understand I've lived my entire life through books and wherever my imagination took me. I spent a lot of time alone and in my imagination when I was growing up. It's where I still live in my head. My daydreams simply manifested verbally, when I was semi-conscious."

"That's a dressed-up way to say you fantasize about me. Not that I'm complaining."

"My mother would call it one of my flights of fancy."

"Indulge me with a 'for instance' of your flights of fancy."

"Promise not to laugh?"

"I'll give it my best shot."

"I sometimes dream about flying around the world in a hot air balloon with a cat named Bartholomew."

"I like it, and it makes sense. You're yearning for freedom from everyday responsibilities that keep you grounded. You want to spread your wings and fly, so to speak. Cats are self-sufficient, for the most part, and they represent independence."

"You're analyzing again."

"Am I wrong?"

Janae shrugged noncommittedly then took another sip of wine.

"Tell me something you want that's attainable. Not a daydream or fantasy."

"That smacks of Carl Jung."

"What do you mean?"

"It means you aren't the only one well-read on the topic of human behavior. Carl Jung said, *Who looks outside, dreams. Who looks inside, awakes.* You aren't at all subtle with your couch-therapy."

"All right. You got me on that one. So, look inside yourself and awaken."

"I don't want to. You'll analyze it into something ridiculous."

"I won't."

Janae lifted a shoulder non-committedly.

"Okay, then I'll tell you my deepest, most innermost desire. I want to live out my life on the Quinlan ranch with lots of kids coming and going and the love of my life is right there with me sharing every minute. Could be our own kids. Could be foster kids. Might be kids on school breaks or on probation. Doesn't matter. I'm just a simple, old fashioned guy at heart, and I don't want to grow old alone. I want the happy-ever-after fairy tale of love and marriage and a baby carriage."

Janae swallowed wrong trying not to laugh at his silly rhyme, which enhanced his goofy grin. Secretly, she wanted a version of the same dream except the thought of having her own children scared the daylights out of her. The older she got, the more she devoured happy-ever-after stories in her leisure time, but she couldn't bring herself to admit it to him now for fear he'd make fun of her for being a shameless sycophant or just plain insincere.

"Fantasizing about being with me is why you came here yesterday, isn't it? It's also why you stayed last night."

"Since you've figured this all out, why don't you tell me? You know you want to."

"All right, I will. I think you fantasized about making love, but when the opportunity of actually acting on that fantasy presented itself, you opted to keep the fantasy over the real thing."

Janae half-shrugged. "Or maybe I was well aware that my two, short-lived intimate relationships didn't last because they lacked the proper foundation, and I've learned from those mistakes."

"By foundation, you mean creating a friendship based on mutual respect and similar life goals before moving into the bedroom."

"Yes. Fantasies are safe. I told you I like being safe. Fantasies don't hurt your feelings or disappoint you. Fantasies can continue unless the fantasy is shattered with reality. No one likes rejection."

Owen nodded. "True. The thing about relationships is they all start somewhere. I think your unlawful entry into my apartment is as good as any."

Janae smiled in spite of herself. "Are you suggesting we are embarking upon a relationship?"

"Why not? Everyone has a first date. Ours is particularly memorable."

"Please don't tease about this."

"Tease about what?"

"Us. We're so different. You're outgoing. I'm not. I'm a research librarian who reads scholarly works and reviews them. I want to be a novelist. My life is in books and words. I don't know anything about rodeo. Rodeo is your entire life. I'm a city girl who will always live in the city. You're from the country, and you're returning there soon. We have different tastes in music and food—"

"Whoa. Hold on. Those are excuses, not reasons. We won't know how much we have in common until we spend more

time together. There's no reason we have to rush into anything."

Skeptical, she ducked her chin and frowned at him. "You're
serious."

"Why do you think I'm not?"

Janae waved her hands over herself. "Look at me. I'm a
mousey, unassuming book worm with near social phobia. I
can't possibly be your type."

"You're selling yourself short. My type of woman is intellectual. She doesn't need a man to take care of her. She can
take care of herself. I'm sorry you don't think you're attractive.
You have a simple, natural beauty. Your kind of beauty shines
on the outside, because of the beauty within your heart. Your
intelligence is part of what makes you attractive. You have
compassion and a moral center, or you wouldn't have been
concerned about my relationship with Laurel before you knew
she was my sister."

Janae barely breathed for fear of losing this moment. No
one—no man—had ever spoken to her like this.

"Will you take the risk?"

"On what?"

"Me. Us. You and me. We'll take it as fast or as slow as it plays
out. What do you say?"

Those words brought all of her fantasies about Owen Quinlan racing toward her at full speed.

Slowly, she nodded while her brain worked to form the word
she couldn't believe she was saying, "Y—yes."

"Good. That's settled."

"Now what happens?"

"We'll swap phone numbers."

"That's reasonable. Then what?"

He shrugged. "I don't know. Eventually swap apartment keys."

"Mightn't that be moving a bit fast?"

"I said eventually." His eyes gleamed with mischief.

Janae giggled. "Going out on dates won't work for us."

"At least, not often, anyway. There's always TV and movies, but even those have their limits. Ordering in and cooking are options."

"Yes. On the weekends, when you're up to it, we could walk to the museum."

"We could do that." Absently, he looked around the room. "Do you play cards? Board games?"

"Yes. I noticed you do, too. And puzzles."

"I'm not crazy about puzzles, but it helps pass the time...at times. Last summer, my nieces and nephews often spent a day or overnight with me, hence the games." He gestured to the shelf. "That came to an abrupt halt once school started. I read a lot. When I get caught up on my reading, someone in the family brings me a new batch of books."

"I can help with providing books. Tell me the genres and authors you like, and I'll bring them whenever you want."

"I appreciate that."

"I suppose finding common interests to spend time together will be part of the fun of getting to know each other."

"That's a good way to look at it."

"I hate to be abrupt, but I really must go. Thank you for supper and the wine."

"My pleasure. I'll walk you home."

"What other chivalrous things do you do?"

"I open doors for women and throw my coat over puddles so they don't get their feet wet."

"You have such a peculiar sense of humor."

"Gotta find a way to survive the challenges and hardships life dishes out, so why not laugh and poke fun right back?"

They talked as they walked to her apartment.

"When you get to work tomorrow, it'll be the first time your coworkers see your face. What'll you tell them?"

Janae thought for a few moments. "The truth. It's outrageous enough they'll believe it."

"That gives me an idea. I should take a picture of you, so we'll always have this moment to remember."

"Don't you dare—" Janae bit off her words. A smirk came to her lips. "Maybe you should. I want a copy. That way I'll always have it to hold over your head when you get too full of yourself."

"Me? Full of myself? You must have me confused with someone else." His laughter echoed along the hallway.

They reached her door, and she unlocked it.

Janae said, "I had a nice time. Goodnight."

"Goodnight." He turned to leave.

"Owen." Butterflies fluttered in her stomach. She couldn't believe she was brave enough to act on impulse.

"Yeah?" He stopped and looked back.

Janae took hold of the front of his shirt with both hands, rose up on her tiptoes, and kissed him. "Now that we have our first kiss behind us, we can anticipate the second one."

"That wasn't much of a kiss."

"But it was enough, nonetheless."

Chuckling, he said, "Goodnight, Janae."

"Goodnight."

Chapter Eleven

Janae put her book away and looked out the window at the Rocky Mountains as the airplane made the descent into Denver. Her thoughts drifted over the days spent with her family. It had been a mostly stress-free visit with only a handful of tense moments when her mother had pushed a little too hard in her attempts to guilt Janae into moving home or had been a little too nosy asking about Janae's personal life. Still, she was a little sad when her parents saw her off at the airport, but not that sad.

Gavin had prearranged with her parents that he'd pick her up at the airport, and she was so glad he had. It gave them private time to talk. No sooner had they hugged, than he'd stepped back to look her over, his face beaming with sheer delight at the sight of her.

"Janae, you are positively glowing. Love looks good on you."

"I can say the same about you. We haven't seen each other in seven months and look at us."

"Harris and I are moving in together New Year's Eve. Isn't that the most romantic thing? We are madly in love. I can't wait for you to meet him."

"I couldn't be happier for you. I won't say I'm in love with Owen, but I'm terribly fond of him. No one in the family knows about him, though. We want time to get to know each other before our families get involved."

He zipped his fingers across his mouth. "My lips are sealed."

Gavin had marveled at the lengths she and Owen had gone to in order to protect their privacy, which included Roger and Margo watching out for them. They'd had a couple of close calls, but had successfully managed to conceal their relationship from Owen's family.

On the drive to her parents' house, Janae had carried on about how she and Owen had hit it off right away, which had put Gavin in stitches at her unintended pun. She'd told him of their loose dating schedule of playing a board game on Wednesday evenings along with soup and sandwiches in her apartment. Friday evenings were a movie and supper ordered in. Saturdays were walks in the park or to the museum after their morning swim. Saturday nights they cooked supper together, then played cards, usually a long version of *Gin Rummy*, which often lasted into the wee hours. They swam Sunday mornings and brunched afterward, then she kept the rest of the day for herself to prepare for the coming work week. She told about their excursion to the Rodeo Hall of Fame Museum in Colorado Springs, which she'd been skeptical about at first, but had, surprisingly, enjoyed.

Gavin had *oohed* and *aahed* when she talked about Owen cooking her favorite meal on their one-month anniversary. Owen had also sent a sunflower and chrysanthemum arrangement for the occasion. She was carefully drying each of the flowers to keep as remembrance. Thinking about those flowers now brought happy tears to her eyes. It was the first time she'd ever received flowers from anyone.

She'd admitted to Gavin that sometimes she wished she and Owen had already moved beyond dating to the bedroom. Gavin, in his practical approach to everything, was of the opinion they were better off taking it slowly just as they were doing. Sleeping together too soon had its special complications. While she didn't disagree. she did wonder if Owen hadn't made those overtures because his doctor had advised against it. Gavin being Gavin had rolled his eyes and told her straight out there was nothing preventing *her* from making the first bedroom move. Why didn't she simply ask him?

That question hadn't strayed far from her thoughts since. Why didn't she?

Margo picked Janae up at the airport in Janae's car, and they stopped at a grocery store for Janae to buy the few things she needed before going to the apartments. She was on her second trip to her car for groceries and her luggage when Laurel and Owen pulled up in a four-wheel-drive pickup. The tingling sensations of an impending anxiety episode coursed through her body at the realization she was caught like a rabbit in a snare. There was no avoiding meeting Laurel.

Owen got out of the pickup and wrapped her in his arms before she could say hello. His kiss of *welcome home* was of an intensity they'd never shared.

"How was your flight?"

"F—fine."

She wanted to believe she was breathless from his kiss not because she was a bundle of nerves under Laurel's disapproving scowl over the top of her sunglasses. Despite being glad to see Owen, Janae wanted nothing more right then than to run up to her apartment sanctuary.

"Laurel, this is Janae. Janae, my sister, Laurel."

Janae nodded politely and extended her hand. "I'm pleased to meet you."

Laurel didn't reciprocate the greeting.

"Be nice," Owen warned.

"I'm *always* nice." Laurel gave Janae a thorough study. "Your face looks better than the first time I saw you. I've never known Owen to be violent toward women. I can't help but wonder if you brought that out in him."

Janae wilted.

"I said, be nice." Owen tossed his duffle and apartment key to Laurel. "Be useful instead of bitchy. I'll help Janae then meet you in my apartment."

Laurel glared at him, but walked toward the front doors without further comment.

"She obviously doesn't like me."

"It seems that way, but it's not. You know how your parents hover over you? Well, she's my helicopter. We're Irish twins—three days shy of exactly one year apart. Ever since I broke my back, her hovering has gone into overtime." Owen carried Janae's two reusable shopping bags, and they made their way to the doors then up the stairs to her apartment.

"Mostly, I ignore her, but I also enjoy egging her on. It's so damn easy to ruffle her feathers. Don't take offense with her. She's actually good-hearted and giving."

"What have you told her about me?"

"Nothing other than the circumstances of blacking your eyes. That's why she's pouting. She's hounded me to find out about you. She enlisted our sisters to grill me, but the more insistent they are, the more fun it is to not tell them. She's hopping pissed at me, but she'll get over it. You can imagine how the three of them were busting at the seams the whole time I was home."

"What about the rest of your family? Have they pressed you for information about us?"

"The whole family's curious, but the more they prod, the less I tell." Owen followed her into the kitchen and put the bags on the counter. "Hey, come here. Let show you how much I missed you like I mean it this time."

Her anxiety about Laurel temporarily disappeared with the warmth of his mouth on hers. It was so good to be in his arms.

"You've never kissed me like this."

"I can say the same for you."

Janae stepped back to look at him. "Five days apart and no phone calls evidently made our hearts grow fonder."

"Apparently, so. I'd ask if you have plans for this evening, but I won't put you on the spot. You have work first thing in the morning, and you need time to recuperate from being gone."

"Let's have a glass of wine, at least. I want to hear about how traveling that far went for you."

"I want to hear about your visit, too. What time?"

"Six?"

"Here?"

"Yes."

A few minutes after he left, Janae realized she'd left her toiletry bag in her car and went down to get it. After chatting with Roger on the way back inside, they parted at the bottom of the stairs, and she continued to the second floor. She was halfway up, when she met Laurel.

Laurel slowed, then came down two steps before she stopped.

"So, you're the one."

"Pardon me? The one what?" Janae hated her disadvantage of having to look up at Laurel.

"Don't play coy. He's in love with you."

Janae's heart pounded. "Has he said that?"

"No, but I can tell. He won't talk about you no matter how much I nag him. I saw you leaving his apartment that morning. I know you slept with him. Your black eyes were a nice touch. He's not violent, and how you prodded him to hit you isn't important. What is important is how well it worked for you to snag him because of the guilt he feels over it. He's financially set. No doubt that was part of your motive. Congratulations. You're slick."

"N—no. You're mistaken. I'm not after his money. I have my own—"

"Save it." Laurel took a step closer and leaned in with a hard glare. "Be careful with my baby brother's heart, sweetie. I never forget, and I don't forgive easily."

Laurel brushed past Janae, then turned and said, "When you go crying to Owen that I hurt your feelings, understand that I don't care."

Laurel was out of sight when Janae's legs gave out. Roger eased into her view, looking between Janae and the front door, then he came up to eye level with her.

"I heard all of it. I stayed close in case she got physical. You okay?"

Shaken, Janae managed to say, "Yes. I'm all right."

"I'll walk you up." At her door, Roger said, "You pay no attention to her. Owen's a keeper." He patted her arm. "And so are you. You're worth twice the likes of her. Don't let her chase you off."

Absently, Janae thanked him. She closed her door and rested against it while her racing thoughts and pounding heart slowed. Then an epiphany hit her like a blast of cold water from the shower head.

For the first time in her life, she had more to lose through avoiding confrontation than in facing it. The realization was both liberating and terrifying. Laurel was wrong that she'd go crying to Owen. She'd tell him, because keeping secrets had a way of coming back to haunt a person, but she wouldn't ask Owen to intervene.

Next time, and Janae had no doubt there'd be a next time, she'd somehow find the courage and quick-thinking to stand up for herself. It was going to take more than a jealous sister to chase her off.

Chapter Twelve

A week after Thanksgiving, a snow squall hit Denver mid-afternoon bringing with it gusting winds and whiteout conditions. Having never driven on snowy streets let alone during a near-blizzard, Janae left the library thirty minutes early, foregoing her weekly shopping for another, less stormy, day. She puttered along, muttering self-encouraging words with her fingers clamped around the steering wheel.

She came up on the apartment parking lot abruptly, pressed the brake too hard, and overshot the driveway in a skid. Backing up the few feet, she maneuvered into her parking spot. Coat hood pulled up, workbag and purse straps slung crossways over her body, Janae ducked her head into the storm, and marched toward the front doors. Out of habit, she glanced at Owen's windows. No light. Odd, considering she could see the snow-masked glow of lights in other apartments.

Margo opened the door for her, and she entered the lobby in a swirl of snow. Janae stamped her feet, pushed back her hood, and generally shook off the snow and cold.

"Thank you. It's a mess out there. The visibility is so limited. I just kept driving and hoping no one was stopped in front of me."

"I'm glad you made it safely. It looks awful."

"I didn't see Owen's lights on. Is he gone?"

"Yeah. He left around two- thirty. He said his therapy had been switched to three o-clock. Funny thing is, it was partly sunny and sixty degrees when he left. We both commented on what a beautiful December day it was. If I was him, I'd take a taxi or call someone. He knows you or me or Roger would be glad to go get him."

"Knowing Owen, he's determined to walk back on his own."

Margo clucked her tongue that she hoped not, but she said, "You're probably right."

Janae went to her apartment and checked for a note or messages on her cordless and cell phones. No messages. A flicker of impatience touched a nerve that if Owen had a cell phone, she could call him and find out where he was. Instantly, she chastised herself for finger-pointing. She was in no position to criticize considering she rarely carried her cell phone as her passive-aggressive way of letting her mother know she wasn't at her absolute beck and call.

After changing into warmer clothes, she went upstairs and let herself into Owen's apartment. She flipped on the light switch. The room was clean and tidy as usual amid its vaguely organized disarray of paintings and photographs. She looked for a note. Didn't find one. She reasoned he'd anticipated being back long before she got home from work and shopping. She checked the time—four thirty-five. Concerned, but not worried, she stood at the window overlooking the parking lot staring into the wind-driven snow that swirled and blurred headlights.

With an appointment at three, followed by an hour of therapy, then twenty or thirty minutes on a clear day to make the walk one way, he should reasonably be here by now. But it wasn't a clear day. It was a blizzard. *Stop it! He's a grown man. He can take care of himself. He very well might have called a cab. He'll show up any minute.*

She checked her watch. Four forty.

Even if she could find the number to his rehab clinic to ask when he'd left, it was probably too late to call now. A thought came to her that he might have called her apartment after she came up here. Out the door she went and abruptly stopped. Backing up, she stared at his heavy coat hanging on the coat tree. What had Margo said? It was partly sunny and sixty degrees when he left. That meant his only defense against the cold and snow was his denim jacket and his cap.

What if he was on his way from therapy when the storm hit? Surely, he'd find a store or building he could get inside and then call her. But he hadn't called. He must be stranded on the street. What if he was so cold he couldn't go on? What if his back or his leg—

She grabbed his coat and took off for her apartment, her need to find him stronger than her better judgment warning of the dangers of driving into a blizzard to look for him, or that her chances of finding him were slim.

Her only phone message was from her mother, which she ignored. She snatched up her keys, threw on her coat, and went to her car. She had a vague memory of her dad saying to crack a window and keep both the heater and defroster off so the inside of the windows wouldn't fog up.

Owen always walked to and from rehab along Colorado Avenue, which she pointedly avoided on her way to work because of the interminable constant stop-and-go waiting for the busy avenue's unsynchronized lights. Right now, she regretted not being at least passingly familiar with Owen's route.

Her car headlights on dim and emergency flashers engaged, Janae scanned a steady rotation from straight ahead to the sidewalk on her right to the center rearview mirror and both side mirrors. Windshield wipers swishing on high did nothing to improve visibility, but it seemed appropriate to have them slapping rapidly to keep time with her racing pulse. Her fear of driving in snow and in the dark disappeared in her search for Owen.

"Where are you? Owen? Where are you?"

Five stoplights behind her, she was the first car at the next red light. The headlights from a car turning across traffic at the intersection shined and reflected like a lighthouse beacon in an ocean of snow, illuminating objects she couldn't see otherwise.

There! Something tall and dark against the building!

She rolled down the passenger window and leaned as far across the seat as her shoulder belt stretched. The headlights of a second car turning shined directly on a man huddled into a recess in the wall.

"Owen!"

Janae made an immediate right turn and pulled up on the slope of the handicapped curb corner like it was her very own parking spot. Her car jolted to a halt when she shoved the gear shift in park before the wheels stopped rolling. She jumped out and ran to Owen.

"Owen! Owen! Oh, my gosh! I found you!"

She put her arm around his waist and half-dragged him the few feet to her car. The wind and snow fought against her to open the passenger side door. Even though the seat was still pushed back from their last outing to accommodate his long legs, Owen had to work to get his right leg bent and into the car, which he barely managed a moment before the wind tore the door from her grasp and slammed it shut.

Janae got in the car and reached into the back seat for Owen's heavy coat. "Here." She mother-hen tucked his coat around him. "You must be half frozen."

"I've been colder, but not by much."

She waited for a car to go by, then she backed up, chanced a tight U-turn, and went through the intersection on a yellow light. She turned again onto Colorado Avenue and drove toward the apartments.

"What happened? Why didn't you stop somewhere and call me? I would have come for you a long time ago. Your leg isn't working right. What's wrong with it?"

"Too cold to talk."

Nodding that she understood, Janae concentrated on driving. This time, she didn't miss the turn into the parking lot.

"I'll get your cane or crutches—"

"No. You be my crutch."

"Put your heavy coat on—"

"Leave it. Sooner we get inside, sooner I can get off my leg."

The slow ordeal of fighting the storm to get inside the building left Owen leaning against the wall, eyes closed, his face tight with pain, and his chest heaving from the exertion.

"You're in no condition to make it up the stairs. We're taking the elevator," Janae said. "No arguments."

A little smile touched his mouth. "Yes, ma'am."

Chapter Thirteen

T he elevator door was halfway open when the electricity flickered. Janae quickly put her back to one of the doors to keep them from closing. The instant hey stepped into the hallway, the lights went out and cloaked them in momentary darkness before the eerie glow of red emergency lights kicked in.

"Whose idea was it to take the elevator?" Owen teased.

Janae made a face at him. They made their way to his door where darkness surrounded them again once they were inside.

"I'll wait here," Owen said. "There are a couple of flashlights in a kitchen drawer. Left side of the sink."

From memory, Janae made her way to the kitchen and hurried back with two flashlights illuminating her way.

"Now what? Couch? Bed?"

Owen rattled instructions in short, teeth-clenched, breathy bursts. "Bed. Change into warmer clothes. Heating pad— Damn. No electricity. Hot water bottle. Need my meds. Glass of water and something to eat. Cookie or cracker. Handful of cereal." He grimaced on a low groan. "Gotta lay down."

Janae pulled back the bed covers then got out sweats and a t-shirt from the dresser. "Do you need help changing?"

"Pull off my shoes. I can get the rest."

"All right. Are you sure you don't need help?"

He shook his head.

"I'll be right back with your medication." Over her shoulder, she said, "Thank goodness for gas stoves. I'll get the water boiling and fix us a quick meal."

With pain pill and muscle relaxant, chocolate chip cookies, and glass of water delivered to Owen, Janae worked by flashlight and stove burners to heat water, warm a can of soup, and cook grilled cheese sandwiches. She filled the hot water bottle and took it to him, then went back to the kitchen. A few minutes later, she carried a serving tray into the bedroom, and sat with him on the bed while they ate.

When they finished, she asked, "How is your pain?"

"Starting to let up some. The food, tea, and meds are doing the trick."

"Oh, good. Now, tell me what happened. Why didn't you call from somewhere?"

"I started out fine. The wind and snow weren't so bad when I left rehab, but I could tell it was going to be a real howler real soon. I pushed myself harder and faster with every step. It hurt like hell. I was pulling and stretching muscles that hadn't worked right in months, but I was steadily moving along at an easy, sort of limping, jog. I haven't been able to do that on a treadmill, yet. My confidence that I could make it the rest of the way gained steam. Then, I stepped off a curb I didn't see coming. I went down in the intersection where you found me."

Janae shuddered.

"All that jolting and pushing my leg to the limit must have set something loose in my back or with a nerve, because my leg seized-up with a deep muscle charley horse that cramped from my foot to my hip. I dragged myself out of the intersection and over to the side of the building. I knew where I was then. Barton's liquor store was at the other end of the block. All I had to do was get there, and I'd go in and call you.

"But I couldn't take another step. Hell, I couldn't go anywhere." He squeezed her hand. "I've never been so glad to see anyone in my life when you showed up. You must have been scared driving in the dark and snow looking for me."

"I was scared, but not for me. For you. I was so afraid you needed me, and I wouldn't be able to find you, and you'd—" Her voice caught, and her eyes filled with tears.

Owen tugged her hand, and she scooted up to kiss him.

"Thank you."

"You're welcome."

"I regretted not having a cell phone. Odd thing, though. The feeling's coming back in my leg. For the first time since I broke my back, when I wiggle my toes, I can actually feel them moving. How about that? Maybe pushing myself did me more good than physical therapy."

"Or the nerves coincidentally reached the healing tipping point."

"No. I don't believe in coincidences."

"Maybe it was a bit of both." Janae took the afghan from the closet shelf, wrapped herself in it, and returned to the bed. "I hope the electricity comes on soon. It's cooling off in here fast."

She took his empty cup then he situated himself lower on the pillows, and tugged the quilt up. "Sorry you're doing all the work. I'm getting sleepy. Side effect of the pills and that I'm toasty warm and comfortable with the hot water bottle."

"You don't need to apologize. I recall a night when you took care of me."

"Yeah, I did, didn't I?"

"I don't think it's a good idea for you to be alone tonight. Do you have anyone who can stay with you? Co-worker? Someone here in the building?" Janae delighted in repeating the words he'd said to her.

Owen smiled a sleepy grin. "I have made a special acquaintance."

"Oh? Does she happen to live in the apartment directly below?"

"She does."

"I'm sure she'll be glad to stay here and watch over you. She's spent a few nights on the couch. I think you'll find that as far as couches go, it's decent for sleeping."

"Did I say that? What was I thinking? This bed's got plenty of room for two." He patted the mattress at his side.

Janae laughed lightly. "Room or not, you're about thirty seconds from dreamland."

"Come to dreamland with me."

"No. You need to sleep."

"Janae... don't leave." He slurred the words and groped clumsily for her hand.

"All right. Just for a few minutes."

She turned off the flashlight and lay beside him, arranging the afghan around her. Within seconds his breathing became easy and regular in sleep.

It was too early for bed, but without electricity there wasn't anything she could do work-wise. It was warm and cozy lying beside him. It didn't take long before her eyelids grew heavy. She'd burned the midnight oil to stay on schedule every night since returning from Ohio, which was always a drawback of taking time off. Although her body relaxed, her mind raced with her usual anxieties and questions in the twilight half-awareness in the moments before falling asleep.

They'd been seeing each other just shy of two months. Was that long enough to know how she felt about him? Did she love him, or was she merely attracted to him, because he was unlike any man she'd ever known? *Could* she love him? That was the real question. He led such a dangerous life, and it frightened her for him and for herself.

What was she to him? Was she merely helping him pass the hours, days, and now the few weeks until he moved back to the family ranch? Would he pack up his belongings one day and leave all thoughts of her a hundred miles behind? Her eyebrows knitted. Those seemed like song lyrics she'd heard somewhere. No matter. What if he asked her to come along? How could she fit into his rodeo life, into his world, when it was so foreign to her?

Drowsily, she saw herself back at Thanksgiving talking to Gavin about her relationship with Owen. He was admonishing her about driving herself mad with useless what-ifs. *You don't have enough information to worry about that, yet. Let things develop without worrying them, and yourself, to death,* he'd said. Then her half-waking dream shifted, and Owen was telling her *Life shovels out enough heartache and puts obstacles in our way on its own without us deliberately adding more.*

Owen mumbled her name, which brought her more awake. Smiling, she snuggled in closer. The last thing on her mind as she went to sleep was how nice it was lying there beside him. She sighed, contentedly imagining herself being with him for the rest of her life.

Chapter Fourteen

O wen spent the ten days of the National Finals Rodeo glued to the television watching every moment. Despite his disappointment of not being there in person, his interest was no less intense, maybe even more. Janae's work responsibilities, and that she was scheduled an extra day at the library each week of December to meet end-of-year deadlines, kept her mostly cloistered in her apartment. They rearranged and altered their date nights to accommodate her schedule.

The few minutes Janae watched of the televised rodeo action was with a morbid fascination that people willingly chose to engage in such a dangerous sport. She cared less about the danger to the human participants than she did for the welfare of the animals.

"Owen, I have to say this. How is rodeo not banned? The events bother me. It seems cruel and inhumane for the animals."

"You're not the only one who sees it that way."

"But you don't."

"No."

"I think you're desensitized to it."

"I'm not. I just know more about what goes on before, during, and after the rodeo. All you see is the few seconds the animals are in the arena."

"Then enlighten me. Help me understand."

Owen thought for many moments. "All right. I'll tell you how we run our business. We specialize in the Brahman breed or Brahmans that are crossed with a different breed to get the weight and size we want. They run free on our ranch, meaning they aren't corralled. We raise some of the supplemental feed, but purchase most of the feed. We make sure they get the nutrients they need to stay healthy and strong. We have a veterinary facility on the premises. In addition to our local vet, veterinary programs from all over send students to us for experience."

"What is a bull's life expectancy?"

"Ten years, give or take a few. They retire when they're done bucking."

"Sent to slaughter, you mean."

"No. They retire to pastures for breeding or they're used in bull riding schools and bullfighting and rodeo clown training programs. We're not in the breeding business, only the training aspects."

"Why don't you breed them?"

"Tending cows and calves is a full-time profession and requires a different kind of ranch. We sell the bulls to breeders and buy young stock back from them."

"When you explain it like that, it doesn't seem so bad for them."

"It's not."

"We do the best we can for the animals. Bulls are an investment, and we protect that investment. Our reputation depends on how well the bulls perform, which means how well they buck."

"What does that mean?"

"A bull that's a keeper—a money-maker—has a strong leap, deep plunge, and wicked spin combined with its natural aggressive character and innate desire to buck. These are the bulls that riders hope to draw. A good bucker means a better chance the cowboy has to place in the money.

"In exchange for eight seconds of top performance, bulls are rotated and get plenty of rest between rodeos. We can't make money with abused, neglected, or unhealthy bulls. You know how you have to regularly take care of your car in order for it to run in tip-top condition?"

"Yes."

"It's the same with bulls or horses or any rodeo stock. Bucking bulls are athletes in their own right and are treated as such by veterinarians and by us as their owners and trainers. A bull that makes the cut to perform at the National Finals Rodeo is worth upwards of fifty thousand dollars, and that's on the low side."

"Fifty. Thousand. Dollars? For one animal?"

"Yeah."

"How much money does your family have?" She slapped her hands over her mouth, her eyes wide with mortification. "I'm sorry. That was an awful thing to ask. I shouldn't have just blurted it, but fifty thousand dollars for one animal is beyond my comprehension."

"It takes a lot of money to run an operation the size of ours. Some of the family takes a regular paycheck, others work the back side of rodeos to make them happen. Some take a percentage of proceeds from rodeos and sales of animals. Running a rodeo stock contracting business is more than providing the animals. Some contractors supply all the stock animals. Others, like us, specialize in one type of animal. We're a little different in another aspect, because we also provide—for a price—rodeo equipment and the people to run and organize a rodeo. We typically negotiate for a percentage of the ticket sales and sponsorships.

"As a point of interest, my sisters and I have secondary sources of income to fall back on. Our parents insisted we go to college and come out with an employable degree. Laurel's got her Bachelors RN. She works a few shifts a month at our hospital. Dana's got a business and marketing degree. Ashley has an accounting degree."

"That's wise of all of you to protect yourselves financially." Janae frowned, her thoughts still with the welfare of the bulls. "Back to what you said about the bulls being well cared for and used to people. Other than their natural desire to buck, it seems to me they have little incentive to buck unless it's to get away from artificially induced pain or discomfort."

Owen nodded that he knew where she was going. "No doubt you've read bulls are tortured to make them perform."

"Well, maybe not tortured, but certainly made uncomfortable. The ropes tied behind their front legs and their hindquarters have barbs and they're tightened to cause pain, so the bulls buck to get away from it. And cowboys hurt them with the spikes on their spurs."

"Yeah. I've heard that propaganda. Rodeo, as an entity, has rules for animal welfare. I can only speak for our personal standards that are higher than any others in the business. To address your concerns, the rope around the bull's hindquarters is called a flank strap. It's a flat strip of leather with a layer of fleece on the underside. The flank strap annoys the bull much like your sock going down into the toe of your shoe annoys you. As far as causing pain, it doesn't. Think of what it feels like if your belt is too tight. It doesn't hurt, but you want it off as quickly as possible.

"The rope around their girth is a specially designed rope for the rider to hang onto, kind of a saddle horn without the saddle. It's a braided rope with a cowbell attached to it as a weight that helps the rope fall free from the bull when the ride's over. The cowboy uses resin on the part of the rope they wrap around their hand to create a stronger grip. Most of the time, that extra wrap comes free when the rider releases his grip. Occasionally, it doesn't, and the cowboy gets hung up."

"You're saying the cowboy deliberately ties himself to the bull?"

"Yes."

"And when something about that goes wrong, that's when you come to his aid."

"Just one of many times during any ride."

Janae shivered and made a face. "What about the spurs?"

"It's true that cowboys rake the bulls' shoulders with their spurs to irritate them, but the spurs have dull, rounded rollers—rowels. Spurring the bull can give the rider extra points, but it's not required like it is in bronc riding. It's called mark-out. Bulls have thick, tough hide. It doesn't hurt them."

"Regardless. I don't like it. If nothing on the bull hurts them, I still don't understand why they go to all the effort to buck."

"When you're naturally cantankerous and it's bred into you to be aggressive and your belt's too tight, and there's a man sitting on your back, and your socks are bunched in the toe of your shoes, you get pissed real quick, and you're determined to make everyone around you pay for it."

Janae laughed. "That's funny when you explain it like that. It's a form of classical conditioning. The harder he bucks, the sooner his discomfort ends."

"That's a good analogy."

"You said you make them tame enough to be around, but you contradicted that by saying they're innately aggressive and cantankerous. How do you reconcile those?"

Owen nodded, smiling. "My tame and your tame are two different concepts. We handle them from calf stage, so they're used to people. That means we can handle them from the ground and load and unload them safely. A tame bull lets us move him from pasture to pasture without charging us. A tame bull doesn't fight the chute when he's vaccinated or getting a medical checkup. He doesn't throw a fit in the truck when he's hauled. Tame in bull language means not always vicious. But I never turn my back on them."

"It just seems to me rodeo animals are exploited for human entertainment."

Owen shrugged in acquiescence. "That's a common criticism."

"Aren't you going to try to convince me I'm wrong?"

"Nope. It's not my job to convince you one way or the other. We're a small slice of the livestock industry, which is constantly criticized in that regard. I'm not making excuses, but rodeo stock have more freedom than dairy cows and racehorses."

"You could stop. Your family could change their line of work."

"You're right. We could." He shrugged in acquiescence. "But we're not going to."

"This really, really bothers me, as in this is a significant issue for me."

He shrugged. "I don't have an answer for you."

"I feel as if I'll have to compromise my beliefs in order for us to stay together."

"Not at all. Compromising one's beliefs creates resentment. Each of us has to be true to what we believe in. There's no other way to live with yourself. Life is a matter of sacrificing and negotiating to make living as enjoyable as possible."

Owen took hold of her hands and played his fingers with hers. When he lifted his gaze, he looked at her for so long that she started to squirm under his scrutiny.

"Hang in here with me a while longer. Hold your concerns and judgments until after you've been to the ranch and met everyone. I want you to see what we do there. See for yourself how it's set up. Look at the bulls. Then attend a few rodeos with me, so I can explain what's going on. I want you to see everything about it. Hear it. Smell it. Feel the excitement in the air. Denver hosts *The National Western Stock Show* every January. This year, I think it runs the eighth through the twenty-third, or thereabouts. I'd like you to go with me."

"Oh, yes. I've seen advertisements for it. It's a huge event in an indoor arena."

"Then you also know there's more to it than just the rodeo. As a family, we take off the middle of December through the end of January, sometimes all of February, depending on the weather. We attend the National Western Stock Show as spectators. It's pleasure, not business.

"We'll walk around the coliseum and look at the exhibits and the 4-H animals and take in events that aren't part of the rodeo. What do you say? Will you humor me? Give it a try at least once?"

Slowly, she nodded. "All right. I can do that."

Chapter Fifteen

Owen enjoyed their date nights at his apartment, but he looked forward to the evenings in Janae's apartment more. This apartment building wasn't his home. It was a temporary abode that was preferable to living in a rehab facility or a hospital room. It was a means to an end. He was living here to get better, to heal, to be able to resume his former life, and every day he worked hard to achieve that goal.

This particular Friday evening, they ordered from a new-to-them restaurant. He'd walked the several blocks to and from Barton's liquor store to pick up Janae's favorite wine just for the occasion. He let himself in, closed the door, and stood there taking in the contrast between her apartment and his, while considering what exactly it was that he liked so much about being here.

Janae's apartment was everything his wasn't—homey, inviting, relaxing, and personal. It was pleasing visually with her décor and aromatically with its subtle hint of sandalwood incense. Always, there was music in the background, noticeable yet unobtrusive in a soft, aurally soothing way. The neat stacks of library books, the carefully arranged books on shelves, the wall hangings and pictures, the bits of memorabilia, trinkets, and knick-knacks were an eclectic collection of her life and her historical interests, particularly the World War II era.

Whenever he commented about how comfortable and inviting it felt to be in her apartment, she was quick to deny possessing domestic skills in one breath, while also refuting any suggestion that this was her home. She called it temporary lodging until she purchased a house.

She was wrong about this apartment not being her home. The area rugs to the curtains and everything in between were an extension of her personality—warm and quiet and friendly. Only the loveseat and matching chair were new. Every other piece of oak furniture had a family story, from the old-fashioned rocking chair, whose origin was traced back to the early 1900s, to the Hoosier cabinet, which functioned as an entertainment center. The cabinet's pull-out work table had *Kansas City Casket and Furniture Co.* written in black grease pencil on the bottom side.

The table had three leaves and six wooden chairs. Two of the chairs she used in other parts of the apartment and the table's leaves were stored due to the table taking up too much space otherwise. Her computer desk was a cut-down library table. The buffet held her Currier and Ives dishes and glasses and the gold flatware in the velvet-lined case, none of which she used. Her four-poster bed and dresser with rectangular mirror and the cheval mirror had been passed down to her, also.

Her apartment was arranged simply and without clutter. The only thing that didn't appeal to him was how heavy the furniture and all the books would be to move, and he was sure glad his back gave him an excuse not to be a part of it. That was for moving companies to handle.

Something was different tonight, though. He looked around, didn't see anything out of place. It smelled the same. No music. That's what it was. He also didn't see Janae. Normally, she met him or greeted him from another room.

"Janae?"

Her arm came up in a wave from the other side of the high-backed loveseat that faced away from him.

He hung his coat up then walked to the front of the loveseat where he found her sitting scrunched and cross-legged and hugging a pillow.

"What's wrong?"

"I just got off the phone with my parents."

"From the looks of you, I'd gauge your level of anxiety is fifty on a ten-point scale."

"They're flying out here for Christmas. My grandparents are coming with them."

"Both sets of grandparents? That's great. I'll be glad to meet them."

"No. Just Grandpa Andy and Grandma Evie. They are fascinated by the Old West and cowboys. I don't think there's a western movie they haven't seen. I mean, I enjoy some of those old movies, too, but my gosh, there are just so many syndicated cowboy reruns a person can tolerate. And no, there's nothing great about them coming here." She inhaled a shuddering breath. "Not only don't they know about us, I was going to meet your family at Christmas for the first time. I've been looking forward to that."

The more upset she got, the faster she talked, and the higher pitched her voice went.

"I've been working myself toward telling my parents about you—about us. Gavin knows, but I swore him to secrecy. I should have told them at Thanksgiving. I know. But I just couldn't face their criticism of what you do for a living."

Eyes filling with bright, ready-to-spill tears, she rushed on.

"Mother wants to stay here instead of a hotel. When I told her my apartment is too small for all of us, she did what she always does and blew me off like I was twelve years old. It will be cozy, she said. Owen, I can't deal with all of them in my apartment even for a few hours let alone several days. There's one bathroom and one bedroom. This loveseat folds out in a bed, but I'll still have to buy an air mattress—"

"Hold on. Hold on. We'll figure this out."

Janae wiped tears.

"When are they coming in?"

"The afternoon of the twenty-third."

He nodded, thinking. "Leaving?"

"Noon on the twenty-seventh." Janae inhaled another shaking breath. "It's such short notice. How will I get them here from the airport? My car is too small for all of them and their luggage. I'll have to make multiple trips or they'll have to take a taxi. What will I do to entertain them? We can't all go anywhere together in my little car, and we can't just sit here with nothing to do. It's such a mess." Janae buried her face in the pillow.

Owen continued nodding as he thought through the situation.

"All right. First off, call and tell them you've got it all worked out. Also tell them about me—not details—just that we've been seeing each other for a couple of months."

"They'll want to know why I didn't say anything about us at Thanksgiving."

Owen shrugged. "Tell them the truth. We weren't ready to get our families involved. Be vague. They'll be intrigued."

"All right."

"After you've talked to them, I'll call my mom and sic her on your mom. She'll offer your parents and grandparents an invitation they can't refuse to spend Christmas at the ranch, so we can be one big happy family or some such razzle dazzle. By the time she's done, your mom will think it was her idea to start with. Plus, your mom can pump my mom for information about me, instead of her giving you the third degree."

Janae sniffled and wiped the tears on her cheeks. "Okay. But there's still the problem of my car."

"That's an easy fix. I'll arrange for a vehicle from the ranch. You'll pick them up in it and bring them to your apartment for just the one night. Your mom will get what she wants, and you'll make your point that there's not enough room for all of you here. It'll be fun. You'll see."

"Fun for you. You'll be in your apartment, and I'll be here," she said drily.

Owen grinned. "I'll take everyone out for supper then you'll drive us around to look at Christmas lights. Then... I don't know. We'll grab milkshakes on the way back here. I always say, when the going gets tough, the tough go get ice cream."

"You say that, do you?" Janae gave him a deadpan look.

Owen laughed. "Next morning, we'll load up early, head out, stop at a pancake house on the way, and get to the ranch by noon. Weather's supposed to be decent. We'll show them around the place. Maybe saddle up a couple of horses for them to ride. My family will keep them captivated with stories about rodeo and ranching. Time'll go fast."

"What about going back to the airport?"

"Someone in the family will follow in your car, and we'll swap vehicles when we get there. We'll stay with them until they board. And all the while, I'll charm them with my glib tongue, witty turn of phrase, and impeccable manners."

Janae made a face. "Really? Glib tongue, perhaps. Impeccable manners and charm? That doesn't resemble you in the least."

Owen laughed. "Don't worry. It'll work out just fine."

Chapter Sixteen

Owen hit the speaker button on the phone. "Hello, Dana."

"I'm returning your call. What's up?"

Stepping back to look at the painting he was working on, he said, "I need to borrow your Suburban."

"Why? Your driver's license is suspended."

"It's not for me. It's for a friend."

"Friend?"

"Yeah, the friend I'm bringing to the ranch for Christmas."

"Why didn't I know about this?"

"Because I haven't told anyone yet, but plans have changed. You'll meet her this weekend."

"Is she the floozy Laurel met and that you won't talk about?"

"What?" He stared at the phone.

"You heard me. You were so stubbornly evasive at Thanksgiving, that you left us with our own conjecturing. Every time Laurel went to see you, she snooped to find out if you've got a woman staying with you."

"Laurel must thrive on disappointment." Owen laughed.

"She says she's seen the same woman twice and talked to her once. She's deduced the woman is a city girl who lives in your apartment building. She described her as cute and timid. Laurel's convinced the woman's trying to get her claws into you for your money and a share of the company—a gold digger. Jenny, Jackie, Janice—"

"Janae?"

"That's it. Now that we've established there is, in fact, a woman in your life, albeit a mysterious woman, why have you kept her a secret?"

"I'm not keeping— What did Laurel say about seeing her, exactly?"

"Just that the first time she saw her, she was leaving your apartment early one morning. The kind of early from spending the night, and that her eyes were purple and swollen like she'd been punched."

"Damn it. It was an accident. I didn't— Did she tell Mom I punched her?"

"I don't know, but if you did, you're going to catch holy hell when Mom and Dad get a hold of you."

"Laurel needs to mind her own business and stop making up stories. That's how shit gets started."

"I agree, but you know how Laurel is with you. Especially after the Kathy episode."

"What the hell are you talking about?"

"Obviously, you and Laurel have some issues to address."

Annoyed, he said, "Yeah, looks like."

"Why do you need my Suburban for two people? Doesn't Janae have a car?"

"She does, but it's too small. Janae's parents and her maternal grandparents are unexpectedly showing up for Christmas.

It's a tricky situation. I'll explain some other time. Janae and I will make a fast trip home this weekend to get your Suburban and leave her car. Probably make it there around noon Saturday, spend the night, and head back early Sunday."

"I can save you the trip. Ashley and I are driving in to Denver tomorrow morning to do some shopping. We could drop off the Suburban and meet Janae. Hint. Hint."

Owen chuckled. "Thanks for the offer, but Janae'll be at work."

"What does she do?"

"She's a research librarian and acquisitions book reviewer."

"Ooh, an intellectual woman. I like her already. Bringing her home to meet the family is a serious move for you."

"Don't go there, Dana."

"I don't have to. You went there on your own. It's evident you're smitten. Want me to let everyone know you're coming, or are you calling them?"

"Go ahead and tell Ashley and Laurel then the three of you can spread the word. I'm waiting on a call back from Mom so I can tell her and ask her to run interference with Janae's family."

"Interference, how?"

"Invite them to spend Christmas at the ranch."

"Oh. All right." Dana was quiet for several seconds. "Owen, speaking of Mom, she and I think it's time to have a heart-to-heart with you."

A cold rush of apprehension scuttled along his arms. "What do you mean? Is something wrong? Is someone sick? Mom? Dad?"

"No. Everything's okay. I meant, it's time to talk about your plans once you get your medical release. We were going to talk to you at Christmas, but with Janae and her family coming, I'll go ahead and tell you now. This is probably going to blindside you regardless of when or how we bring it up."

"Blindside me with what?"

"We don't mean to tell you how to live—"

"Yes, you do. I know all you females better than that. Get to the point."

"We think you need to reassess your priorities. You're missing out on some things that will slip clear away if you're not careful."

"Such as?"

"Such as a family of your own. Owen, you're a kid magnet. You need kids before you're too old to enjoy them. Look, we all know you're living for the day when you're back in the arena, but you have to face the possibility that it's over for you."

Owen's silence dragged on.

"Say something."

"Thanks for not blindsiding me."

"Don't be a smart ass. I'm serious. The Quinlan bullfighting training program is solid. You're turning out some of the best clowns and bullfighters in the profession."

"But...?"

"We think it's time for you to really dig into developing the rodeo camp. You know Tony's been fired up about it ever since you ran the idea past him. With his own close call in the same rodeo when you got hurt, then another one in Phoenix, he wants to live long enough to see his boys grow up. You two aren't getting any younger, you know. Shawn and Gabe have some ideas on it, too."

"You make it sound like we've got one foot in the grave."

"Look. All I'm suggesting is you think about it. Really think about where you want your life to go and how you're going to get there, while you're physically able to."

There was no more avoiding his deepest fear. Dana had laid it bare, and he couldn't ignore it.

"Owen, are you there?"

"Yeah."

"Think about it, okay?"

"Okay."

"All right. I want to ask you something personal."

"You can ask."

"You've never introduced any of your girlfriends to the family. I mean, girlfriends outside of the rodeo crowd that we pretty much already knew. Is Janae, maybe, the one?"

Owen debated what to say.

"Never mind. You don't need to answer. Your hesitation says it all. I'm happy for you, and I can't wait to meet her. See you Saturday."

"Yeah. Saturday."

"Love you."

"Love you, too."

Owen walked to the window and stared out at nothing in particular, just staring and thinking. He wanted to help kids whose life circumstances had started them down the wrong road. He also wanted a family—a wife and children. The longer he was with Janae, the more he felt she could be that wife. She was kind and generous, deeply thoughtful, and intelligent, and absolutely endearing in so many other ways.

But she'd told him right off she didn't want children. On an intellectual level, he understood and accepted that. Emotionally, he was at odds. She wasn't keen on his rodeo life, either. Even without injuries, time and age would take him out of the arena, but he wasn't ready to quit yet.

Janae was right. Everyone has issues. He'd denied his up to now. Dana made him face himself honestly. His blind spot was denying the possibility that his career as a rodeo bullfighter had ended last spring. He was scared he was a has-been, just another rodeo casualty with his glory days behind him.

He wasn't ready to give up his rodeo life. He had to know, and he knew with the certainty of the sun going down in the west, that once he had his medical release, he'd go back to bull-fighting to prove to himself he could. Would once be enough? Could he walk away then, or would he continue to crave just one more time? Would Janae still be in his life knowing he was facing two thousand pounds of death every time he stepped into an arena? Could they find middle ground on her aversion to rodeo and his hope for a family?

He shook off the gray clouds of the what-ifs and maybes and unanswerable questions. The fact was, someday soon, he'd be back in the arena. No amount of conjecturing, wishing, or worrying would change whatever happened after that.

Chapter Seventeen

After spending an hour with his parents and grandparents, Owen spirited Janae away from his parents' house to give her the space she needed to regroup before supper and meeting the next round of family. Janae drove them the half-mile along a narrow road that Janae complained was hardly more than a two-track cattle trail to his house. The low bottom of her car occasionally scraped the higher rise of the dirt and grass running along the center of the crude road.

He had her park on the concrete slab in front of the garage. The house was built into a hillside, perched on top of a concrete foundation with double garage doors spanning more than half the width and a regular door on one side.

Janae got out of the car and looked it over.

Owen walked around the front of the car and half-reclined on the hood. "You've got a funny look. What's wrong?"

"Nothing's wrong. I'm surprised. No, that's not quite it. I'm bewildered, caught off guard."

"Why?"

"My assumptions and my preconceived notions have been challenged."

"What assumptions and notions?"

"Where you live in relation to where your family lives." She gestured behind them. "There are eight houses situated around a common center that must be... Oh, I don't know, six or eight city blocks square. It's like a mini community in the middle of nowhere. Each house has its own style. The way they're landscaped creates an interconnected commonality of a neighborhood, yet they're also private."

"Real estately speaking—"

"That's not a word."

"Sure it is. I just invented it."

Janae just shook her head.

"My grandparents set it up this way with an eye to the future."

"The future?"

"In case descendants sell the property. The houses, outbuilding, barns, and corrals are on 160 acres—a half section. Each house sets on its own legal-description lot. The full section is legally divided into lots. It takes the argument out of how to divvy up the land if or when the time comes. As for being a little community, that was on purpose, too, in case we ever wanted to plat a town here. The rest of the property is grassland with some alfalfa and corn acreage."

Janae nodded, considering his explanation in silence.

"There's something still bothering you. What is it?"

"It doesn't bother me, *per se*. It just strikes me odd that your house is completely separated from the others."

Grinning, Owen said, "I've always been the outlier in the family."

"Evidently. I assumed you lived in one of the family houses where it's more...civilized."

That brought a chuckle from Owen. "I did, but remodeling got under way a year ago in order to upgrade all the houses with the latest conveniences, new carpets, replace cabinets, and all that. It was the right time for me to bring in my own house."

Janae continued nodding and looking at Owen's house.

"There's still something you're not saying."

"It's just not what I expected. It's a house partially stuck into a hillside. No landscaping. No trees."

"Barren? Ugly?"

"Yes." Janae cringed and wrinkled her nose. "I'm sorry. It's rude of me to criticize. I'm sure it's lovely inside."

Owen laughed. "No need to apologize. It is barren and ugly, but you're right about the inside. Everything's new and shiny. The only reason it's not finished on the outside is because I haven't been here to do it.

"The house is a prefab that I ordered to my specifications. I had it set on the concrete garage-basement foundation last April. The landscaping and getting the whole thing bricked was put on hold when my broken back threw a wrench in my plans. All the crews were ready to go, and there were plenty of family and friends offering to finish it up. But there are some things I want just so, and I need to be here to oversee it. The bricklayers start work in March, and the landscaping crew will show up in the middle of May."

"You should take pictures of before and after," Janae said.

"Good idea. I'll mention that to my nieces and nephews. They'll have a heyday outdoing each other to see who can take the best and most pictures."

Owen opened the hatchback and hauled out their bags. Janae glanced at them, then looked again.

"Does this mean I'm not staying at your parent's house?"

"Did you really want to?"

"No, but everyone will think we're sleeping together."

"They already think that. Would it be so bad if we were?"

She made a face and a half-shrug.

With a grin and a quick kiss, he said, "Didn't think so. Let's go inside. If it makes you feel less licentious, I asked my mom to have two bedrooms set up. Nothing fancy, just functional. Mattresses on Hollywood bedframes and probably not the most comfortable you've ever slept on. I doubt there's even a table or dresser in the rooms."

When he flipped on the light in the garage, Janae saw cardboard boxes stacked off to the side of what seemed like an area large enough for a fleet of vehicles.

"How many vehicles do you plan to park in here?" she teased.

Owen gestured. "Just two up here at the front. Eventually, there'll be a wall put in about two thirds of the way back to make a storage area. Those boxes hold the sum total of my personal possessions."

They went up the circular staircase to the main floor, which brought them out on the far side of the carpeted living room. He dropped their bags and looked around.

"Feels good to be home."

"It smells fresh for being uninhabited all these months."

"My mom loves me. She's kept it spotless."

Janae eyed him. "Granted, I've only been around your mother a short time, but that doesn't seem like her."

"Okay, I confess. I pay my nieces and nephews to come in every week and give the place the once-over as well as little kids can. They feel like they're helping, and they make a few bucks. I asked my mom to give it a good cleaning for us. Air it out.

Knock down the cobwebs. Check the water heater. Turn up the thermostat to take the chill off. Stock the cupboards and fridge. Put out a flower arrangement on the dining table. You know, the usual."

"I hope you thanked her. That was a lot of work."

"She hired a cleaning service. They sent me the bill. I might be the baby of the family, but I was never coddled."

Janae laughed. "Did she hire your shopping done, too?"

"No. She didn't mind doing that. I'm sure my grandmothers went shopping with her."

"So... This is your home," Janae mused.

"It will be when I move back. Have a look around. Tell me what you think."

"What do you mean? Think about what? It's brand new. I don't have to look around to see how nice it is, although it needs furnishing. The folding table and chairs and TV trays are quaint in a bachelor sort of way, but..." She cringed.

Owen chuckled. "Yeah, I know. I need to get some real furniture. I'm fond of big old oak furniture. Furniture with a family history." He cut her a side-eye, his mustache moving around an almost grin.

"Is that a veiled reference to my furniture?"

"Just an observation that there's room here for big furniture. I think a piano would look good on that wall."

"*Hmm.*" Janae worked not to smile.

"Go on. Look around. I'll check the cabinets and fridge."

Janae took her time wandering in and out of rooms. The house itself was on one level. She poked her head in each of the four adequately-sized bedrooms—two on either side of common hallway with a bathroom between each pair, a master bedroom and adjoining private bathroom with double walk-in closets, the living room and kitchen was one large area with a rolling bar and barstools providing a divider of sorts. There were plenty of kitchen cupboards and counter space.

The door over the garage was double dead-bolted to discourage anyone from stepping out and taking a steep drop to the ground. That door and the two on either side of the house suggested a balcony and veranda would be built and added around the perimeter. A wide glass patio door on the west offered a splendid view of the snow-capped Rocky Mountains beyond the broad prairie.

She ended her perusal at two adjoining rooms. One was empty. The other held what seemed to her to be Owen's entire life displayed in plaques, frames, or trophies, and she read the writing on each one: *Barrel Man Award, Bull's Eye View Award, World Champion Bullfighter, Bullfighter of the Year, American Rodeo Cowboys Association Freestyle Bullfighting, Extreme Challenge Bullfighting* along with evidence of corporate sponsors from beer to off-road vehicles. It reminded her of a shrine honoring his rodeo life.

Separate from that array of awards and achievements was another display of framed photographs of Owen with children of various ages who were clearly rodeo participants. A poster with hand-signed names hung above the pictures with a marker-written statement in the center of the poster: *Thanks from all the 4-H and FFA members for hosting the rodeo camp.*

It was as impressive as the gallery of awards in his parents' house showcasing the contributions from the Quinlan family for their long history as rodeo stock contractors who had consistently provided the highest number of top five hundred ranked bulls over the past fifty years. With stark clarity, Janae realized Quinlans weren't just a rodeo family. They *were* rodeo. Owen, in his profession, was among the elite. When he'd said rodeo was in his blood, he hadn't been speaking metaphorically.

Hearing Owen greet someone, she made her way back to the living room to see three women shedding winter coats and generally making themselves at home. Laurel was one of the women, and she didn't smile when she saw Janae. One of the other two women came right to her.

"Obviously, you're Janae. I'm so glad to meet you. I'm Dana, the middle sister."

"I'm glad to meet you."

"I'm Ashley, the oldest. We couldn't wait until you and Owen came back for supper to meet you."

"I recognize you from the times you've visited Owen. I also recognized your parents and grandparents, too."

Ashley asked, "When, or maybe, how, did you see us?"

"My apartment is directly below Owen's. Our corner windows let us see the parking and courtyard."

Ashley laughed. "No wonder we never encountered you. You saw us coming."

Dana shot her brother a pseudo-frown. "That's kind of underhanded, don't you think? She knew who we were before she came here."

"It's your own faults. I know how you three are. Janae and I wanted time to ourselves without our families sticking their noses in our business."

Dana and Ashley laughed. Ashley said, "You're absolutely right, we would have."

Janae anticipated the awkward silence and didn't let it happen despite her stomach churning from remembrance of the one time she and Laurel had spoken.

"Hello, Laurel. It's...nice to see you again." Inwardly, she cringed at her unfortunate hesitation.

"I can't say the feeling's mutual."

"That's not very hospitable." Owen fixed Laurel with a hard gaze.

"Sorry, it's the best I can do given the circumstances."

"What circumstances? This is an introduction."

"The circumstances of you having your head up your ass and ending up with a broken back the last time you hooked up with a city girl. What the hell are you doing with another one? And why the hell would you bring her to meet the family? You know she doesn't have what it takes to live our kind of life."

Dana's mouth fell open.

Ashley scolded, "Laurel—"

"It's okay." Owen crossed his arms and studied Laurel for many moments. "Janae told me about your confrontation at the apartment. She also asked me to not get involved. I respect that. It was between the two of you, until you just dragged me into it. Say what you have to say, and say it straight, Laurel."

"Have you known me to say it any other way? Bullfighting is dangerous enough when you're in top form. You don't need some pretty piece of ass messing with your mind or compromising Tony or Gabe or Shawn when they're depending on you in the arena."

"What the hell are you talking about?"

"The chicks you attract. You haven't stayed with one long enough to learn her middle name."

Owen turned to Janae. "What's your middle name?"

Janae stammered, "Am— Amelia Marie Evelyn Louise...." Her voice faded, and she shrugged apologetically. "My grandmother's names."

Chapter Eighteen

Owen did a *you've got to be kidding me* double take, then turned back to Laurel. "Janae Amelia Marie Evelyn Louise Palmer." He shot Janae another glance and shook his head, although his eyes shined with amusement.

"My point exactly." Laurel's expression was as smug as her tone.

"Cut the crap. What's really on your mind?"

"Kathy Landon."

"What about her?"

"Excuse me." Janae pushed past her flight instinct to hold the shaky ground she stood on in this skirmish. Striking her own blow, she said, "I resent that your judgments about me are based solely upon your perception of a woman from Owen's past. I've given you no reason to dislike me. None whatsoever. Yet, you accused me of wanting him for his money. I don't need any man's money. I am financially secure in my job, and I will come into a substantial trust when I'm thirty. *Substantial.*"

She punctuated the word with ducked chin and her shoulders set in her eye-to-eye stare-down with Laurel.

"And furthermore, I'm not just a pretty piece of ass. He's going to find out I'm the best piece of ass he's ever had."

As soon as the words left her mouth, hot embarrassment coursed through her body, but she held herself staunchly determined not to crumble in front of Laurel or break eye contact first.

Owen stared at Janae for several seconds then slapped Laurel on the shoulder, chuckling. "Well, sis, um... While I can't confirm or deny what she said, I am more than willing to find out."

Ashley laughed. "Oh, Janae, I like you. You're quick."

"Are you saying you two haven't slept together? You've been seeing each other since September." Dana looked at Janae then at Owen.

"October 12th," Janae corrected.

Owen grinned. "Traditional family values and all that."

"Yeah, right." Laurel scoffed. "You didn't have traditional family values on your mind when you were with Kathy."

"You're not going to like where that accusation takes you, Laurel. Tread carefully."

"That sounds like a threat."

"Not a threat. A warning that you're digging a hole for yourself."

"Oh, no. You're not getting out of this. Remember Guymon? Of course you do. Tony got stomped by that bull. Gabe got banged up, and you broke your back. Shawn wasn't supposed to be working, but he went in when you three went down. All because *your* head wasn't in the game. It was in bed with Kathy."

"You're wrong, Laurel. Kathy'd been seeing Jeff Evers for a year or so. They had a fight and broke up. We hooked up. Then she and Jeff got back together in February during the week I was in Tucson. Kathy was in college in Kansas, so it wasn't unusual for us not to see each other for a couple of weeks at a time. She flew in to the Clovis Rodeo and showed up at the restaurant where a birthday celebration for a friend was going on. She dropped the bombshell on me that she was pregnant."

Laurel gasped. "What? You have a child? That's a shitty secret to keep—"

Owen held up his hand to silence her. "She said the baby was Jeff's. I retaliated with demanding a paternity test. Words were said. Accusations exchanged. She slapped me and walked out. She'd kicked the shit out of my pride in front of friends. When I cooled off, I knew the baby couldn't be mine, which made my irrational resentment even worse. By the next day, I felt pretty lousy for making the paternity allegation.

"Guymon was the next time I saw Jeff. Kathy was with him, and she was wearing a diamond engagement ring. My pride was still stinging, and my resentment had turned to full-out jealousy. I hadn't had much use for Jeff before, and I had even less then.

"He caught me behind the chutes and came right out and admitted about him and Kathy getting together while I was in Tucson, and that it was a lousy thing to do. But he blew it off as no big deal. No hard feelings. Shit happens, you know."

"Oh, wow. That was ballsy," Ashley said. "What did you say?"

"Say?" Dana said. "I would have punched the sanctimonious s-o-b."

"It took all I had not to punch him. I said cheaters deserved each other. I didn't shake his hand. I walked off. People witnessed our confrontation. It clinched the rumors of bad blood between us over Kathy."

"Owen. Stop. I get it. You don't have to justify yourself."

"You started this, Laurel. You're going to hear the rest of it."

Owen pinned Laurel to the spot with a hard, icy glare. It took Janae's breath to see it. She wanted to look away, fade into the background, be anywhere else in the world right then. But, like his sisters, she was rooted there, dreading to hear more, yet hanging onto his every word.

"Jeff is new to rodeo. Couple of years. He's a better bronc rider than bull rider. Not champion-decent, but he places high enough to pay his entry fees and probably makes gas money. He's the type who holds to the saying if you can't make it to eight, hang-up and thrill the crowd. I've seen him pretend to get hung up on a bull and a bronc just to get the crowd on their feet and applauding. He's put more than one of us in danger because of his grandstanding.

"That day in Guymon, he'd drawn a hell of a mean bull, and he rode him to the buzzer. He'd tied his hand down tight and his glove was caught in the rigging. He was hung up for real this time. I saw what was going down before the buzzer, and I was already on the move. In that split second, a whole lot of things went through my head. *That fast*." Owen snapped his fingers.

"I realized I hadn't been in love with Kathy. Oh, I'd loved her all right, but I wasn't *in* love with her. I hadn't known there was a difference until then. She loved Jeff. There was no way he was going to die on my watch and leave her to raise a child alone, and I sure as hell didn't want her to turn to me to be a second-choice father.

"I jumped up on that bull with Jeff, hanging off the side, yanking and working the rope loose, and all the while that bull was twisting and turning to get us on the ground. Tony was in front distracting him every way he knew how, just like he always does. Then the bull hooked Tony and flipped him under his feet. Stomped him out cold. Gabe was in the middle of it dragging Tony out of the way when the bull swung his head and hit Gabe full on the chest. He couldn't get up, but he kept crawling toward the fence, dragging Tony with him.

"I got Jeff loose, and he hit the ground running for the fence. Somewhere in the melee, Shawn showed up and teased the bull away from the pickup riders trying to help Tony and Gabe. That's when the bull saw me, and I made a run for the barrel. The bull hit that barrel so hard it went flying over the fence. He let out a bellow, ducked his head, and charged me.

"I slapped that bad boy on the nose then walked right up his neck and across his back with my eye on my path to the fence or chutes. The bull swapped ends on a dime, hooked my foot as I came off his back end, and threw me in the air. The next thing I remember was waking up in a hospital bed."

Owen looked at Ashley then Dana and, finally, back at Laurel.

"I wasn't distracted in Guymon, and I didn't let Tony, Gabe, or Shawn down. I did my job better than I'd ever done it. I got Jeff loose and distracted the bull after he hooked Tony, which made it possible for Gabe and Shawn to move in and do what we all do best—protect a downed man. I saved Jeff's life despite him pulling the stunt that caused the wreck, *because* he was the father of Kathy's baby. I paid a price for it, so if you want to blame someone, blame Jeff or Kathy. But don't point your finger at me."

Laurel stared at him. "Why... Why didn't you tell us? Doesn't it bother you that people think you're washed-up? That you got hurt because of a woman who—"

"It's none of my business what people think of me. I know who I am, and I know what I stand for. More than that, I know why I did what I did. Some things are best left unspoken and unexplained. No. Don't do it." He raised a warning hand to her. "Don't be looking for trouble where there isn't any. I can see it in your eyes. Don't jump on Tony for not telling you. Leopards don't change their spots."

Laurel bristled. "What are you insinuating?"

"I'm not insinuating anything. I'm saying it right out that there are a lot of things we don't tell you, because you blow everything out of proportion and overreact. You make it worse. Like what you're thinking about stirring up now."

Laurel looked to her sisters for support to refute him and found none.

"He's right," Dana said.

Ashley shrugged. "It's true."

"Did you know about this?"

Both sisters nodded.

Ashley said, "In our defense, we didn't know about the baby."

Laurel sucked in a sharp breath, her eyes wide with realization. "Quinlan— *Quinn*. They named their son after you."

Owen gave her one curt nod.

"I...I don't know what to say." Lauren teared-up.

"How about *I'm sorry*. Janae didn't deserve any of the abuse you've handed her."

"All right, so minding my own business has never been a skill I've mastered. I'll work on doing better from now on."

"Don't make promises you can't keep," Owen warned.

"Really. I mean it. I don't want to be left out anymore." She turned to Janae. "I'd like to have another chance at becoming friends. I'm so sorry for how I've treated you."

Janae took a steadying breath. "Apology accepted."

Owen looked at Janae long and hard. "I've never lost my head, or my heart, over a woman. Until now. I love you." A little smile moved the corners of his mouth. "There. I said it in front of my sisters, so you can take it to the bank. I love you, Janae, even if you do have four middle names."

Chapter Nineteen

J anae was proud of her ability to remember people's faces and their names from meeting them only once. This was a talent that served her well having met Owen's sisters, his three nieces and four nephews, the three brothers-in-law, both sets of grandparents, and his parents all in one evening. She delighted in his parent's names, August and Maeve. The names were quaint and old fashioned. Most of Owen's aunts, uncles, and cousins would join the festivities on Christmas Day.

Everyone had welcomed her as if she'd always been part of the Quinlan family, which eased her apprehension of making it through the upcoming five days of holiday overstimulation with even more of the Quinlan clan there in addition to her family adding to the mix of country and city personalities.

Supper turned into three more hours gathered in front of the fireplace talking and laughing. Janae was captivated by the family stories. She hoped some of the same stories would come up when her family was here. It was close to eleven as she and Owen walked hand-in-hand to his house, enjoying the windless, gentle snowfall.

"My family likes you, if you hadn't already figured that out."

"I like them, too."

"What did you like best about today?"

"Finding out I'm not allergic to cats. Isn't that wonderful? I've always wanted to hold a cat and rub my cheek against its fur."

He chuckled. "You did plenty of that, all right."

"Oh, and playing fetch with the dogs." Janae laughed. "Now, the two guinea pigs Laurel's boys dropped in my lap were a bit startling at first."

Owen laughed with her. "Just think how exciting it'll be tomorrow when you ride a horse."

"Me? Ride a horse? Oh... I don't know. That's pushing the try-new-experiences fun a bit too far, don't you think?"

"You'll do just fine. I'll be right there with you."

"I've had such a good time, but I'm ready for a shower and bed."

"Me, too."

"Race you there." Laughing, Janae took off, then realized in a few steps that Owen wasn't coming. She stopped and turned to wait for him.

He walked to her, his steps slow and measured. "That was hitting below the belt."

"Oh, Owen, I'm so sorry. I wasn't thinking." She reached for him in apology.

"It's all right." He leaned down to kiss her, a grin spreading over his face. Just before his lips touched hers, he took off running with long, strong strides. Glancing over his shoulder, he taunted, "Last one home's a rotten egg."

"*Ah*—You cheater!" Janae ran after him, laughing too hard for any chance of catching up.

Dressed in fleece pajamas with matching robe, Janae passed Owen's bedroom on the way to hers.

"Going to bed? I'm wide awake. How about a movie to fall asleep to?"

She backed up and stood in the doorway, her arms full of her toiletry bag, bottle of lotion, and dirty clothes. "Okay. Good thing we're both night owls."

"These are the latest thing. DVDs." He held one up. "If they catch on, I'll have to replace my VHS player. Ashley picked up a player and half-a-dozen movies for us, since I don't have a TV antenna up yet, which won't bring in much reception anyway."

"What are the choices?"

He showed her one DVD at a time.

"*While You Were Sleeping*. The reviews say it's a delightful romantic comedy. Let me put my things in my room. I'll be right there."

When she returned with lotion and socks in hand, Owen was reclining against the pillows propped up against the wall that served as the headboard. Janae made herself comfortable beside him and proceeded to lotion her feet then put on her fuzzy socks. She pulled up the folded quilt from the foot of the bed and snuggled against him, her head resting on the hollow of his shoulder.

"Aren't you chilly in just your sweats and t-shirt? You don't even have socks on."

"Not right now. Showering always cranks up my internal heater. Ready to watch?"

"Yes."

Cozied-up as she was to Owen, Janae's thoughts didn't stay with the movie. Owen's comment that his family assumed they were sleeping together, and that it wouldn't be such a bad thing if they were, ran through her head. What was it Gavin had said? It wasn't written anywhere that she had to wait for Owen to make the first move.

"Owen."

"Hmm?" He continued watching the movie. When she didn't say more, he looked at her. "What?"

"You told me you loved me a few hours ago. That seems like a pretty significant change in our relationship."

He nodded, but didn't say anything for several moments. "It is."

"I was well aware you were fishing for my approval when you brought me to your house. You have it. It's comfortable here. I like it."

"I'm glad. That makes me feel good. I wanted you to see how I live. Where I live. Where I'll always live."

"I also appreciate that you were considerate of my feelings when you offered me a separate bedroom."

"But?"

"Remember when I went to your apartment to have you turn down your music, and you said I was actually acting on my fantasy of sleeping with you, but that I'd changed my mind?"

"Yeah. I remember." He eyed her curiously.

"I don't want to fantasize anymore."

He tilted his head to see her face better. "We've had plenty of opportunities that we've never taken. Why now?"

"Why *not* now?"

"All right. I'm game. But if you want this to play out like your fantasies, you're going to have to clue me in on the details so I can play along." His eyes shined with amused interest. "All I know is we'll have to pretend your pj's are a black negligee…unless you brought that negligee with you." He wiggled his eyebrows to say that would suit him just fine.

Giggling, she said, "No, I didn't bring it. In fact, I don't own a black negligee. Anyway, what I'm wearing will be moot once I'm out of it."

"I like how you fantasize. What do you want me to do?"

"I want you to lay on your belly, so I can feel the rods and screws in your back and—"

"That's it? You could have asked to do that long before now."

"*Shush.* Don't be such a complainer. I want to feel the hardware in your back while straddling you and covering your skin with Cinnamon Desert Spice Aphrodisiac essential oil."

Owen stared at her for a few seconds then burst out laughing. "That's a pretty specific detail in this fantasy of yours. Did you bring the cinnamon spicy whatever with you?"

Laughing, she said, "No. I read it in a romance novel. I don't know if such an oil even exists. I have lotion, though." She wiggled the bottle. "Vanilla Silk."

"What happens after lotion?

"Anything we want. You're sure it's okay to sit on you?"

"Janae, I broke my back. I wasn't—"

"I know. I know. I heard you. You broke your back. You weren't castrated." Janae lightly thumped his belly, which made him grunt and grin.

"That's right, not by a long shot. Straddle away, but there are two conditions."

"Oh?"

"I want you naked, and I get to undress you." He reached to untie her robe.

Gently slapping his hand, she said, "No touching...yet. You'll get your turn. Me first. It's my fantasy. T-shirt off."

"Not my sweats?"

"Patience, Grasshopper." Grinning slyly, she ordered, "On your belly, mister."

He clicked off the movie and TV then rolled onto his belly. The hallway nightlight provided a soft yellow glow that accentuated the shadowed ambience in the room. Janae pulled the waist of his sweats low, then settled herself over the swell of his hips.

He exhaled sharply.

"Am I hurting you?"

"Not in the way you think. Keep doing more of what you're doing."

"I haven't done anything yet."

"In that, you are mistaken. Go ahead. Press your fingers just off the scar. You'll feel the hardware."

"Oh! I feel it. Are you sure this doesn't hurt?"

"I'm sure. There's no feeling there. All I feel is the pressure of your fingers."

"You said your physical therapist is going to discharge you soon."

"Yeah. Now that the feeling has returned in my right leg, for the most part anyway, and my mobility is nearly back to normal, there's nothing more she can do to help me. I won't quit massage therapy, though. I get stove-up if I miss a session."

"Does your masseuse do this?" She lay prone on his body and slipped her hands low between his belly and the blankets.

He groaned. "No, Brian has never used his method, and I'll be damned if I'll ask him."

"Nor this, I'll bet." She sat up and drizzled a thin line of lotion along the length of his spine.

He squirmed and grunted. "You're right. He's nicer than you. He warms it first."

With upward and outward strokes, Janae kneaded the muscles along the full length of his back and across his shoulders. Leaning low, she nuzzled the back of his neck, delighting in his involuntary shiver.

"Just how tough are you?" she crooned at his ear.

"As tough as they come."

She tugged his sweats over his hips, down his legs, and pulled them off as she scooted to the foot of the bed. He rolled to his back as his sweats hit the floor.

Janae slowly inched her way up his body, lingering and kissing him here and there. "Betcha you cry uncle first."

Her saucy smirk egged him on. "I won't mind at all if I lose this bet."

"There is something before we go further."

"What's that?"

"My fantasies include responsible protection. I don't make love carelessly."

"I don't, either."

"Where are yours?"

"Duffle. Yours?"

"Toiletry bag. Since you don't believe in coincidences, analyze why we both came prepared, Mr. Psychologist."

He chuckled. "Premeditated spontaneity."

"That's not a thing."

"Yes, it is. I just made it up."

Janae laughed. "You should write a dictionary of your made-up words. Don't go anywhere. I'll be right back with our spontaneous not-a-coincidence protection."

He held her fast. "That can wait. Let's play a while first."

"Ooh. I like that. Just one more thing." She straddled his groin. "You need to know I've loved you since that morning I punched you in the belly."

He grinned, "Yeah, me, too."

Slowly, slyly, even a little shyly, she held out the ends of her robe belt for him.

"Now it's your turn. Make my fantasies come true."

Chapter Twenty

J anae didn't see much of Owen once the National Western Stock Show opened at the Denver Coliseum. When they did find time to have supper or a glass of wine together, he went on about how good it was hanging around the bucking chutes and generally getting back into his former lifestyle. Her apprehension about his excitement to be rubbing rodeo elbows again was compounded by how much he was looking forward to returning to the arena himself. Janae kept her misgivings to herself and didn't rain on his rodeo parade.

As she'd promised, she accompanied him to the Stock Show three times. He was in his element showing her around. The crazy amount of people in attendance compounded by the sights, sounds, and aromas were nothing like she'd ever experienced in her life, and the first time left her overwhelmed.

The second time she went, his entire family—grandparents, parents, sisters and spouses, and all the nieces and nephews—were there. They sat together in the reserved Quinlan seats right at the arena railing and near the bucking chutes.

On her third excursion there, she was able to pay closer attention to details and tune out the extraneous noises bombarding her. She even watched events with keener interest and enthusiasm now that she was more educated in the ways of livestock, showmanship, performances, and the rodeo events in general.

She'd not cared at all for calf roping, but the bronc riding was thrilling. Her favorite event was the mounted team of young riders, who performed precision trick riding, roman riding, and dressage. It was an amazing display of teamwork and synchronized horsemanship. She could have watched them for hours.

Tonight was the only time her schedule and the bull riding events had coincided. She pushed back her dread in light of Owen's excitement to have her with him the first time she watched the bull riding in person. She wished for his family's company. His nieces and nephews would have provided a welcomed diversion from her nervousness. His mother empathized with Janae's trepidation regarding bull riding in general, and specifically with Owen's chosen profession. But none of them had made it. The ranch was besieged by a blizzard and roads and highways on the eastern plains were closed.

The announcer asked for the audience's attention. "Folks, we have a few minutes before the bull riding, and I want to take this opportunity to introduce one of the youngest and greatest rodeo clowns—correction—bullfighters, the profession has ever seen.

"His family has been in rodeo for over a hundred years dating back to his great-great-grandparents clear on down to his family today. They've all worked to bring the sport of rodeo to a higher standard, whether you're talking about their consistent production of high-quality bulls, being forerunners in

the humane treatment of rodeo stock, or the level of athleti-
cism and skill all the cowboys and cowgirls in the family have
achieved.

"This young man and his three brothers-in-law are world
class clowns and bullfighters. They have bullfighting and
rodeo clown training programs that bring athletes from all
over the world to learn the trade. Adding to that, many members of the family are emergency medical services providers,
which has saved many lives in the arena."

Janae leaned toward Owen and said, "That sounds like your
family."

Owen grinned. "Get ready."

"For what?"

When a spotlight began scanning the crowd, Janae sank in
her seat. "Oh, no."

"Folks, I'm speaking of none other than Owen Quinlan of
Quinlan Rodeo Stock Contractors right here."

The spotlight found them.

"Owen, stand up and give the crowd a wave."

The crowd cheered and clapped, and one of the clowns in
the arena tossed a wireless microphone up to him.

The announcer went on. "Owen, you're patched into the
P.A. system. We've seen you around here day and night, but
we couldn't get it worked out to catch you in one place long
enough to have you say a few words to the spectators. I know
I'm speaking for everyone here that it's good to see you back
here after your unfortunate accident last spring."

"Hello, Ray. It's good to be back."

"Who's the lovely lady with you?"

Owen grinned and looked down at Janae scrunched low in
her seat, huddled deep into her coat with the hood pulled over
her head. He hauled her up and put his arm around her.

"This is Janae Palmer." Out of the side of his mouth, he said, "Wave and smile."

"Owen, inquiring minds want to know. Any news when you'll be back in action?"

"I got my medical release December 30th. I'm fit to throw myself to the bulls anytime. And I fully intend to." Owen's voice projected loud and clear.

The crowd applauded and cheered.

"Well, folks, you heard it for yourselves. Owen Quinlan says he's back on his feet and ready to rumble."

Janae crumpled into her seat, acutely aware of the continued staring, pointing, and talking in their general direction. Owen mingled with the people who had gathered to see him, which consisted mostly of children who waved or shoved all sorts of objects at him for his autograph—hats, shirts, photographs, programs, pieces of paper, and the white plaster cast on a girl's arm. He patiently posed for the pictures their enthusiastic mothers took.

When he sat down again, he pecked a quick kiss on Janae's lips. "You did good. Overwhelmed?"

"How could you tell?"

"Don't worry. It'll grow on you."

She doubted that, but she managed a smile and weak nod.

Four cowboys into the bull riding, the next cowboy made it to the eight-second buzzer just at the moment when yelling and hollering rose up from the chutes. The sound of crashing metal and splintering wood filled the arena. A metal panel gave way under the weight of a two-ton bull clambering over the top. The connecting panels caved, setting free three more bulls. All four snorted and pranced, on the prod and ready to stomp whatever took their fancy.

Janae shrank farther into her coat, horrified at the sight of the bucking bull and the cowboy on his back who was clearly in trouble.

"*Shit!* He's hung up. There's not enough of them. Someone's gonna get killed."

Owen vaulted the railing before Janae had time to think let alone react. He hit the dirt running and went straight for the hung-up cowboy who dangled and flopped like a rag doll on the side of the bucking beast.

Pickup men moved in. A bullfighter went down under a charging bull's feet. He scrambled up and commenced dodging and antagonizing the bull to lure him toward the chutes. The barrel man played cat and mouse with another bull. A clown ran circles around another bull, dodging and teasing to get the bull to chase him.

All this played out in slow motion before Janae's eyes as if time were standing as still as her heart that seemed to stop beating.

Like a gladiator in the midst of lions, Owen ran and dodged until he made it to the hung-up cowboy. Owen made a grab for the bull rope, clamped his fist around it, and yanked. The cowboy fell free and lay face down in the dirt. Owen swung over the bull's back and landed on his feet. Another bullfighter slapped the bull on the nose with a straw broom to distract him from the downed cowboy. The bull bellowed, swapped ends, and tossed that clown aside with the swing of his powerful neck and head. The clown rolled to his feet and circled around behind Owen, watching for his next opportunity to intervene.

When Owen slapped the bull's nose with his hat, the bull ducked his head, gave out a bellow, and came at Owen with his head and horns swinging. Owen pushed off and walked up the bull's broad neck and down his back. The bull bellowed and swapped ends again, bucking and twisting to get Owen on the ground.

The bull gave a mighty kick and another buck, his hindquarters rising well above his massive shoulders and front legs, which propelled Owen into a mid-air flip. Owen came down solidly on both feet, darted between bull and cowboy as the bull turned and charged. Stepping sideways, his right leg gave out, and he went down under the bull's charge.

Lurching up, Janae heard her own scream as a separate, surreal part of herself, her fingers clenched around the railing, her body flushing cold in frozen horror. The announcer's voice reached her as a roar of incomprehensible nonsense words that her subconscious deciphered as calming the crowd.

Owen somersaulted out from under the bull and took off zig-zag running toward the bucking chutes, which enticed the bull to chase him. Owen leaped onto a bucking chute and crawled like a monkey up a tree to the top with the help of cowboys on the fence grabbing him and pulling him safely from the bull's last hook with his massive horns. Two pickup riders hazed the bull on into the pens behind the chutes, which enticed the other bulls to follow.

Owen was the first to reach the unconscious cowboy. Emergency personnel soon joined him. The ambulance had entered the arena before the bulls were back in the pens. There wasn't a sound in the coliseum until the injured man was strapped on a backboard and loaded into the ambulance. Owen climbed in with him.

"Folks, show these brave men how much you appreciate their work." Ray's voice boomed, breaking the collective held-breaths of everyone there. "Especially for Owen Quinlan coming to the aid of his fellow barrel men, clowns, and bull-fighters to risk his life for the good of others."

The crowd went wild cheering and clapping.

"You all witnessed Owen at his best. It takes the right bull and the right circumstances to see him perform the *Quinlan Climb,* and you saw it with your own eyes right here. Few can do it, and fewer even try. Well done, everyone. Well done!"

Janae sat down hard, her heart pounding, her stomach churning. Her vision narrowed and her ears rang to the point she thought she'd pass out. A cocoon of self-protection wrapped itself around her mind to buffer what she'd witnessed. But the terror left in the wake of witnessing Owen tempting death was too much reality for her to bear.

Owen thanked the paramedics for the ride to his apartment. Janae's car was in her allotted space, which eased his mind for having abandoned her. It was a relief to see she'd made it back without getting lost like she always worried would happen if she drove alone at night. He looked at her windows, saw the familiar glow of the nightlight, and went on inside.

He was halfway up the main stairway, when Roger called from below.

"Hey, Owen. Janae's not here."

"What do you mean? Where is she?"

"She had me drive her to the airport. She was pretty shaken up. Some sort of crisis. She said she had to go home."

"But she didn't say what it was?"

"No. She didn't say much at all. There were tears, but she wasn't crying. Just really upset. She only packed a carry-on."

"Okay. Thanks. I'll give her cell phone a call." Once again, he regretted not having a cell phone.

"Anytime, Owen. Hope everything's okay with her."

"Yeah, me, too. I'll let you know when I find out."

"Thanks."

Taking off his boots just inside his door, Owen hung up his coat, lamenting that his cowboy hat was lost somewhere in the coliseum. He hoped a kid picked it up. He didn't mind so much. It was a small sacrifice for as well as it all turned out. No one had been seriously injured.

He stopped in the kitchen for a glass of water and to put on a pot of coffee, then he stripped out of his dirty clothes as he made his way toward the bathroom, grabbing the cordless phone on the way. His call went to her voice message. When he turned on the bathroom light, seeing a folded paper taped to the mirror gave him a funny feeling in his stomach. He put the phone down, peeled off the paper, and unfolded it to see Janae's small, neat handwriting.

Owen,

You deserve more than this note, but I can't face you or talk to you. You've probably called my cell phone. I didn't answer, because I didn't take it with me. In case you haven't talked to Roger, he drove me to the airport. I told him I had to go home because of a crisis.

There is a crisis, but it's not what you think. It's within me.

I thought I could handle what you do for a living. I can't. We've talked about your rodeo life. I've watched bull riding on television and the recordings you've shown me. But I wasn't emotionally invested. I was separate and detached, because none of it was real to me. I went with you to the Stock Show to try to understand and better appreciate the world in which you live. It was more enjoyable than I'd anticipated. I realize now that was because you were a spectator with me.

What you did tonight...what I saw firsthand...made me face the cold hard fact that I can't live with the worry that every time you step into an arena might be the last time I see you alive or uninjured. I've never loved before you, and to lose you to your mistress Rodeo is too great a loss for me to bear.

I'm not strong or brave, Owen. I'm plain-Jane Janae who hides in my safe world of research and reading and writing. Being with you these past three months allowed me a peek into a different kind of life than I've ever experienced or even dreamed about. I'm better off in my world, and you're better off in yours. I'm so sorry I've hurt you by leaving with only this explanation, but it's all I have to give you. Maybe with enough time.... I just don't know.

I'm taking a leave of absence from work. I don't know when I'll return.

Janae

With her note in hand, he went to the bedroom, opened the top dresser drawer, and took out a small blue velvet jewelry box. He lifted the hinged lid and smoothed his thumb over the Black Hills gold band with nested diamonds. Closing the lid, he placed the box on the dresser.

Running his hands over his face then through his hair, he muttered, "Damn. Just when I'd figured it all out."

Chapter Twenty-one

On their return from a walk in the nearby park, where Janae and Gavin had been strolling for an hour, Gavin noticed the strange car parked in the Palmers' driveway half a block away.

"Your parents have company."

"Oh?" Janae commented absently. "That's nice." Her emotion-saturated mind didn't pay attention until they were close enough to see the license plate. "Michigan? My parents don't know anyone from Michigan. Well, I don't think they do. We don't have family or friends there."

Curiosity momentarily pushed her sadness aside as they walked up to the kitchen door. A man with his back to them moved into view at the breakfast nook bay windows. Then he turned, and she recognized his profile.

Owen. Rental car.

She stopped in her tracks.

"Janae? What's wrong?" Gavin followed her stare.

"Owen's here."

"Oh. *Ohhh*." Gavin grasped Janae's hand as the ramifications of Owen's presence hit him. "No matter how badly you might want to, you know you can't hide from him. Be strong."

He opened the door and nudged her to go in ahead of him. She stepped across the threshold and moved aside for Gavin to come in. She stared at the floor, her hands shoved in her coat pockets, and her shoulders hunched to make herself small and insignificant, which is how she viewed herself since running away from Owen.

"Hello, Janae."

She lifted her gaze to meet his. The raw hurt shining in his eyes pierced her heart with arrows of self-shame.

"Hello, Owen," she whispered.

Vic introduced Gavin to Owen, then he and Ramona motioned for Gavin to go with them to the living room.

Owen continued to look at Janae without speaking, until she couldn't stand the silence or endure the anticipation a second longer.

"Please. Say something."

"I'm always amazed at the conundrums, the surprises and twists, of life." His voice was low, tight. He shook his head and exhaled heavily. "I discovered something about myself last night. I couldn't wait to tell you, but you were gone."

Janae didn't trust her voice or her strength not to cry. She could only nod.

"I found out I didn't need my mistress anymore. When I faced that bull and got the cowboy untangled from the bull rope, I knew I was done with bullfighting. It was cathartic. I'd triumphed over a broken back to go out at the top of my game. I was ready to go in a different direction with my life." He paused as if gathering his own strength to continue. "And when I wanted to tell you—to share it with you—you weren't there."

A sob rose in her throat. She had no words of defense.

"I've been waiting for the right time." He held out a blue velvet ring box.

Janae's heart fluttered. There was no mystery to its contents. She'd never dreamed, never even considered a proposal. She took the box with a hesitant hand and eased the lid open. She caught her breath. This was no ordinary ring. He'd taken great care choosing it.

"I love you, Janae."

She met his gaze. Unfinished words hung silent and ominous between them.

"But...?"

"But you have to make whatever choices are right for you. I've made my choice. I want to marry you. I want whatever future we can have together for however long it lasts—with or without children. I don't care about that. I just want you in my life, whether it's one year or fifty years. I'll never regret one minute of knowing you. Of loving you."

"Even though I ran away instead of staying and talking it through?"

He nodded. "I don't blame you for that. What you witnessed terrified you. Terrified you for me. I get it. I do. You went into emotional survival mode, and you sought shelter in the safest place you knew—back home with your family. I take responsibility for your panic. I didn't prepare you for what you saw. It's second nature for me. I made the mistake of not seeing what I do from your perspective—through your eyes. You once warned me about that...my tunnel vision.

"You saw what the men in the barrels do to keep the cowboys safe. You saw the bullfighters do their magic in the arena. But

I didn't help you process what you saw. I threw you to the lions—bulls—emotionally and psychologically last night."

Her eyes blurred with tears. "I *was* terrified. Terrified for you. Terrified for me. My feelings are all jumbled. I reacted as I always have—with avoidance. I should have waited for you. I regret that I didn't. By the time I arrived here, I was ashamed for only leaving you a note. That was cruel of me. I'm sorry. So sorry…"

"Here." He held out a CD jewel case. "Listen to the last song. I know country isn't your kind of music, but give it a listen anyway. It explains what I've been trying to say to you."

Janae took it, read the list of songs, then looked at him. "*The Dance?*"

He nodded. "It's a song about being in love, no matter how long it lasts, no matter how it ends. It's about the sharing and the memories. It's about experiencing all the metaphorical dances in life we'd miss if we knew of the heartaches waiting in our future. It's about celebrating all the happiness and joys in life, because we don't know when they'll be our last. It's about being better off not knowing what the future holds for us, because if we know when the hurts are going to happen, we won't take the risk of loving and losing."

"Will you listen to it with me?"

"No. You need to listen to it without me."

Her stomach twisted. She whispered around the tight tears in her throat, "You came all this way to say goodbye." Of course this was goodbye. She'd worked hard to push him away.

He nodded slowly. "I don't want to live without you, but the reality is when I leave here, I'll still be that same cowboy I was when we met—the same guy taking risks and living every moment of my life. I've never known any other way to be. But

I thought I'd found middle ground for us to build a life on..." His voice trailed off on a shrug.

"I—I need time. I need to think...to figure out what I'm feeling. I don't know... I just don't know."

He looked at her for a long time. "What I hope is that you won't stay a victim to your fear of living every moment of your life. Don't keep hiding yourself—or your heart."

He held out his arms in a helpless gesture that he didn't know what else to say. "Do whatever you want with the ring. Now that it's not going on your finger, I don't want it. Tell your folks I said thanks for the coffee and conversation. Give my regards to Gavin. Sorry we didn't get a chance to talk."

The kitchen door closed behind him with a cold, harsh click. Her heart urged her forward. She grasped the doorknob, then hesitated when he didn't get into his car. He stood beside it, staring over the roof as if lost in faraway thoughts.

Go to him. But she couldn't move. She pressed her palms and forehead against the window glass and watched him.

In a few seconds, he got into the car. He didn't look at the house. Suffocating hurt, regret, and shame heaved in her chest. Her dad put his arm around her, and she leaned her head on his shoulder. Together, they stared at the empty driveway. Vaguely, she was aware of Gavin and her mom behind her.

"Janae, honey, your mom and I had a long talk with Owen. He arrived just minutes after you and Gavin left on your walk. We're so sorry for how this turned out. We admit we overprotected you and made many mistakes in raising you. The way we sheltered you instead of allowing you to test your wings and learn your strengths on your own is partly what brought you to this crisis in your relationship with Owen."

Vic turned her to face him.

"We didn't help you prepare to deal with life. We made your decisions for you, because we didn't want you to stumble and struggle. That didn't help you. It just made life harder for you to live in when you were older. It took many months, but we did come to understand you moved to Denver to get away from us and our possessiveness. And you know what? We're as sorry about that as we are proud of you for striking out on your own."

"Owen once said I had run away from home when I moved to Denver, and now I've run away again."

With a glance at Ramona, Vic wrapped his arms around Janae, and she rested her cheek on his chest.

Ramona said, "Sweetheart, if we were to ever have a son-in-law, we think you couldn't choose a better one than Owen or marry into a finer family."

"I should have stopped him. I should have told him what he means to me."

"It's not too late," Ramona encouraged.

"Yes, it is. He didn't look back." She drew in a ragged breath.

Gavin took hold of her hand, gently tugging for her to look at him. "Maybe he was afraid to look back. It could be his heart couldn't bear it if you weren't watching him. He wanted to believe you were watching."

Vic kissed the top of her head. "Let's go to the living room and listen to the song."

Janae picked up a throw pillow as she sank down on the couch between Gavin and her mom. Vic put the CD into the player and gave the remote to Gavin.

Janae drew in a shuddering breath as the first notes from a melancholy piano set the mood. The singer's resonant drawl told the story of looking back on life as a dance he'd shared with the person he loved and then had lost. He sang of living life for the memories and never regretting the losses. He sang that the pain of losing someone you love was worth the risk of being left with only memories after that person was gone from your life.

With the last, fading notes, tears streamed down Janae's cheeks. Gavin hit the repeat button, and then put his arm around her and drew her close. The music and his touch opened the floodgate of her despair, and she sobbed into the pillow as her heart finished breaking into tiny pieces.

Chapter Twenty-two

S oftly falling snow accompanied Janae on the nine-ty-minute drive east of Denver to Overland Crossing then another twenty minutes north to the Quinlan ranch. She pulled into the yard and followed the narrow road on past the house. She kept going toward the corrals and barns, drove around behind them, and parked near the covered arena. She got out of her car, zipped up her coat, and walked the few feet to the wide, heavy metal arena gate. Climbing to the top, she swung her legs over and perched on the top rail.

She saw Gabe, Shawn, and Tony on foot talking with a small group of men, which she deduced were there for bullfighting training. Owen was on a horse at the opposite end of the arena. Her insides jittered and churned with equal parts apprehension and anticipation of seeing him after missing him every moment of the longest five days of her life.

Tony saw her. She waved. He caught Owen's attention and pointed toward her. Owen turned and looked at her a long while before riding to her.

"You're a long way from Ohio."

Janae nodded. "I flew in last night. Margo picked me up at the airport."

"Then you know I moved out of my apartment."

"Yes. I wasn't surprised. I expected it. Margo and Roger send their greetings."

Owen offered a slight smile that didn't last longer than a breath. "Why did you come here?"

So many reasons ran through her head. *Because I love you. Because I don't want to live without you. Because I'm so sorry I ran away from you. Because I want you to forgive me for hurting you.* It was a combination of all of them, but each one didn't express what had put her on a plane yesterday to get to him as fast as she could while hoping she hadn't waited too long.

"To tell you I listened to the song."

"And?"

"It *is* better not knowing what life has planned for us. I want to look back on the memories we've made. The happy ones, the sad ones...all of them. And I want every dance in life with you."

"You're sure?"

"Yes. I'm sure."

"Even though I'll never give up rodeo? I'm done with bull-fighting except for volunteering at youth rodeos and training bull fighters and clowns. I'm going forward with developing my rodeo program for kids—"

"*We*. We will. I want to be part of it. I don't know how or what I can do, but we'll figure it out." She read his misgivings in his long, silent study of her. "You want to believe me, but you have doubts."

"I won't lie. I do have doubts."

"Remember the talks we've had about children?"

"Yeah. What about it?" He gave her a suspicious look.

"Four."

"Four what?"

"Children."

He sucked in a sharp breath. "Don't say that unless you mean it."

"And a cat and dog for each child." She worked hard not to smile. It felt good to be the one doing the teasing, even though she was dead serious.

He cocked his head, skeptical.

"Maybe even guinea pigs and hamsters and rabbits. I'm uncertain about lizards and snakes, though." She didn't even try not to smile at how silly that sounded.

"You're serious."

She just looked at him and waited.

True to his flippant nature, he quipped, "We'll have to build on to the house to accommodate all the kids and critters, and the house isn't even finished yet."

"We have a lot to get done, don't we? And the sooner we start on our family, the better."

"A person doesn't just wake up one morning and decide to have children."

"I know."

"What changed your mind?"

"So many things." She plunged straightaway into everything she wanted to say, her words running into each other. "Talking with my parents and Gavin. Admitting that I don't want to live my life alone. Facing myself honestly and admitting how much I loved the man who took a red-eye flight from Denver to Ohio when he could have made a phone call, or not called at all. Envisioning that man as the father of our children." She took a breath.

He looked at her a long time. "Walking away from you was the hardest thing I've ever done." His voice was thick with emotion. "I regret not turning around and going back to you."

Her whisper was wet with tears. "Oh... Owen. Watching you walk away is the hardest thing *I've* ever done. I regret not running out to stop you."

"It won't do us any good to find out after the fact that we can't find common ground. We have a few things to work out before we walk down the aisle."

Her momentary relief that he hadn't written her off as a bad mistake came crashing down when his levity of mere seconds ago vanished like a flowing faucet turning off—there one moment, gone the next.

Tentatively hopeful this wasn't as dire as it sounded, she asked, "Such as?"

"How are we going to blend our lives? I don't expect you to give up your work for me, and you know rodeo is in my blood. You're opposed to just about everything rodeo-related. I don't believe that's changed."

Janae nodded. "I won't deny I'm at odds with what you do and with rodeo in general, but the more I learn, the more my understanding grows, and the more I'm able to let go of *some* of my misgivings. I'm willing to keep learning and to keep an open mind, as long as you acknowledge that I'll likely never completely embrace your rodeo way of life. As for my work and what I want to do in my life, I have some ideas."

"All right. I'm willing to listen to what you have to say—not just hear—really *listen*. I'm willing to keep an open mind, too."

"I also promise I'll always talk to you, no matter what the situation or problem is. *There's nothing that can't be solved with a good laugh, a long talk over a bottle of wine, and a rowdy romp in bed.*"

Owen laughed. "I guarantee I'll love you and our kids like every day is the only day we'll have." He nudged his horse closer, serious again. "There's one more thing we have to clear up. Maybe even the most important thing."

Her breath hitched. What else was there to talk about? Old habits of thinking the worst gripped her.

"Don't you ever think of yourself as plain-Jane Janae again. There's nothing plain about you. Never has been. Never will be. You're done selling yourself short. You're braver and stronger than you give yourself credit for. You've got spunk, beauty, brains, and I'm not going to live another day without you." He sidled his horse up against the fence and pulled her down to sit across his lap sidesaddle fashion. "And I can't imagine any other woman as the mother of our children."

Janae slipped her arms around his waist and held on, her heart full of laughter and her spirit soaring with joy. She brought out the ring box from her pocket. "Marry me?"

Owen took the box and flipped the lid open. He motioned for her left hand and slipped the ring on her finger.

"Well, how about that? It's a perfect fit."

Before she had a chance to admire it, he pulled it off, returned it to the box, and snapped the lid closed.

"Uh— Why did you do that?"

"We determined it fits. Next time I put it on your finger will be when we say *I do*."

His eyes shined with his familiar teasing.

"I hope that's sooner than later."

"Pick the day, place, and time. I'll be there."

"I'm pretty sure my mother will want to have a say."

"As will my sisters and mom."

Janae laughed. "Let them. I don't care about any of that."

"Me, either."

"Then I accept that you accept my proposal. I don't want to look back and regret what could have been. I want the dance with all the memories and all the heartaches. I want the dance with you, Owen Patrick Quinlan. With you."

Brushing a kiss over her lips, he said, "And what a dance we'll have. I promise you that."

THE END

About the author

Native Coloradoan Kaye Spencer grew up on a cattle ranch in northeastern Colorado. Since 1990, she's lived in a small, rural town located in the heart of the infamous Dust Bowl area of the 1930s in southeastern Colorado. Kaye writes mostly western romances.

Louis L'Amour's western novels, Marty Robbins's gun-fighter ballads, and western movies and tv shows inspired her love of the American Old West—truths and myths alike. Kaye's favorite movie line is from *Quigley Down Under*: "I said I never had much use for one. Never said I didn't know how to use it." (This is exactly her relationship with her kitchen.)

During Kaye's younger years, she followed the amateur rodeo circuit and experienced life on the thoroughbred race-track. She even did a stint as a cleaner of sugar beet storage silos (after beets are processed into sugar) to keep down the sugar dust in order to minimize static electricity. Otherwise...

BOOM! She did manage to find less-explosive jobs that put food on the table and clothes on the backs of her three children of which she was their only parent.

Having had enough of 'odd' jobs, Kaye entered college to earn a degree in teaching. The degree landed her a position as librarian for a 90,000-volume children's library. After that, she worked as a teacher of students with special needs, school psychologist, 6th – 12th grades English and history teacher, principal, and director of exceptional student services. Some thirty-five years later, she retired. She is fortunate to be able to spend a lot of time with her family. Many rescued and homeless animals have found a home with her, and more are always welcome.

Learn more about Kaye, her books, and where to find her on social media: www.kayespencer.com

Also by

KAYE SPENCER